As My Sparks
Fly Upward

& Other stories

Matthew St. Amand

Published 2002 by
The Fiction Works
Lake Tahoe, Nevada
www.fictionworks.com

ISBN 1-58124-810-5
Printed in the
United States of America

To Marnie & Paul,

Here is my slice of
Windsor & Dublin.
All the Best,
Matt St. Amand

As My Sparks
Fly Upward

For

John Kennedy Toole,
patron saint of unpublished writers

. . . you're innocent when you dream . . .
—Tom Waits

Contents

Aisling

I have lived in Dublin, Ireland, for two years working as a writer in a publishing company. While my head was turned ordering a pint, as I daydreamed in my cubicle, or while walking home through deepening shades of evening, something resembling my own life took hold here. I'm not a Dubliner; I'll always be "Matchew from Canada" to my friends and co-workers. My flat mates will likely never stop asking me, "Now, Matchew, do you have *that* in Canada?" regarding everything from microwave ovens to pornography and sunshine. Still, there come nights, watching the sun wheeling west—the moon in close pursuit—that I feel a pang of missing, remembrance; find myself consumed by the names of places and people who are past and gone.

It seems I'm most awake during the dead hours of the night, when the wind moves on the shoulders of the ghost-legions lurking along the Grand Canal, when the din of distant drunks rise like jungle-cries; as an insomniac paces the floor above, an argument flares in the flat below, and rain falls everywhere outside. Coming home, glowing drunk, clutching a frozen pizza under my arm, still laughing at stories told around the table at the Gingerman Pub, Slattery's, Mulligan's, my mind reflects and tabulates, guessing backward at years, and names of people I thought I would never forget.

I was born in Windsor, Ontario the summer Marvin Gaye was singing, "What's Goin' On?" A city that gets altogether too much stick for being small and slow and industrial. There's probably no point describing my childhood and adolescence there to someone who faults a small city for not being a metropolis: strumming a battered acoustic guitar in my room, shooting hoops at the schoolyard, roving the neighborhoods with friends all those Friday nights in spring. The beacons of my landscape light with neon intensity: Sacred Heart elementary school, the riverfront, Ambassador Bridge, the Dominion House Tavern, the Grad House pub.

After finishing school I was never more aware of the pang that has always been with me—double-edged and incorrigible: exasperated with Windsor while there, missing it desperately while away—bellowing through my nerves the ancient words God used to banish Adam and Eve, "Gird your loins and get the fuck out!"

So, I moved to Dublin and discovered a truth I thought only existed in fantasy: that a man could live and work and enjoy himself in equal proportion, free from guilt, stain, persecution and undo molestation.

After another night at the Gingerman Pub—where a friend asked me, "Silicon breasts. Now, Matchew, would you have *that* in Canada?"—hearing the shouts of drunks along the Canal, there's no temptation to rhapsodize about home; I am too familiar with Windsor's nicks and dents and frayed seams. Even so, these stories are mine, and so is that city huddled on the Detroit River, watching the water flow past, and life extending all around.

Best Man

Anxiety always leaves me feeling like I've got the flu. It centers in my stomach and spreads its poison in all directions. I've got that feeling today. Bad. My best friend, Dennis, gets married in an hour and I'm the best man—which means wearing a tuxedo, which I haven't done since the senior prom four years ago, MC-ing the reception, which I've never done before, and giving a speech after dinner, which I hope I'll never have to do again. At the rate I'm going with relationships, Dennis will be my pallbearer before he's my best man. It's not that I have no luck with women, my luck is surprisingly good at times—which causes problems when I already have a girlfriend.

"These things should come with instructions," Dennis says, pulling the tuxedo from its plastic covering. We are in his bedroom in his parents' house, empty now except for a single bed and my sleeping bag. *Last* Saturday Dennis and I moved his stuff to the apartment where he and Mira will live after the wedding.

"Have another look in the bag," I say. "Maybe there's a One-Eight-Hundred tuxedo help line."

He grunts and drops the garment bag to the floor.

I pull on the tux pants. Dennis stands motionless, his shirt unbuttoned, trouser fly open, holding a small bag containing brass button covers and cufflinks; seems about to say something, then shakes his head and tosses the bag onto the unmade bed.

"It's not like putting together Mira's exercise bike," I tell him. "You're not supposed to have any pieces left over."

"I'll wait for you to figure out where they go." He sits on

the bed and picks up the rumpled pages of his speech.

And I get thinking about my own speech.

Knowing Dennis for thirteen years—since I was ten and he was eleven—I figured my speech would be simple to write. But as the months leading up to the wedding narrowed to weeks, and the weeks dwindled to days, I found that I had no speech at all. Two weeks ago I sat down and told myself I would not get up until I had at least the first draft completed. I sat for two hours and wrote as many usable sentences. Everything sounded like the start of a bad greeting card. But nerves and writer's block aside there was a larger reason eclipsing all others: I'm against the marriage.

I've felt this way since agreeing to be best man.

What's the problem? I've wondered again and again.

Small things.

Mira moved here three years ago from some numbed little town a few hundred miles north—a move I admired considering she was only nineteen, and had no job prospects. I remember a night, early in their relationship, being on a double date with them at a sports bar. At one point a hard rock song came over the sound system, and Mira took Dennis' hand, cuddled up to him and said, "This will be our wedding song."

She was joking. I know she was joking. But it was more than that.

All of this weighs on me because I like Mira. She has an easy sense of humor that fits well with the running jokes between Dennis and I. She gets along with my girlfriends—often better than I do. But beneath the laughs and conversation, the compass arrow of her need always points back to Dennis.

There was one night my girlfriend, Karen, and I were at Mira's place with Dennis, playing *Balderdash*, drinking beer that Dennis and I made at a brew-your-own club. It was a good time, the beer was better than we could have hoped, but I was distracted most of the evening by Mira constantly grabbing for Dennis' hand, cuddling up to him on the couch, resting her leg over top of his. I said nothing, figuring it was my own hang-up—I've never been much for public displays of affection. The way I see it, people make a big outward show to compensate for what they lack inside. Which explains the fleeting shelf-life of Hollywood marriages. I said nothing about it while driving Karen home, until she wondered aloud how Dennis could stand being *handled* all evening.

I have accused myself of being jealous, being childish and selfish—of being a bad friend—but there's no way around it: Mira's smothering Dennis, having taken him in an emotional choke-hold from the first. And he's done nothing but go along with it. So, over these three years I have accepted the situation. After all, who am I to choose the girl Dennis is to fall in love with? I've little success solving that riddle for myself. Needless to say Karen and I lasted four months. It just didn't work out.

I head into the bathroom across the hall; adjust my tie, check my hair. Stifle a yawn. Finally finished my speech yesterday: typed half at home in the afternoon and wrote the rest by hand while watching TV with Dennis last night. It's short, a couple of childhood stories and a toast to the bride and groom. If I can't be a good sport at my best buddy's wedding, what kind of guy would I be?

Dennis comes to the bathroom doorway. "I can't do this," he says.

"I'll clip your tie, just give me a second."

"Fuck the tie." He goes back to the bedroom. I follow him; my tie still slanting down on the left.

"Take it easy," I say, "The tie's tricky—"

"I said fuck it!"

It takes me a second to realize he's upset—*very* upset. Dennis sits on the bed.

"What're you talking about, then?" I say. "Your speech?"

"The wedding. *Every*thing."

He speaks clearly, I hear every word he says—yet it's like I can't hear him at all. "What?"

"I've been going over my speech," he says, "looking around my room, thinking, 'It'll be empty . . . forever. *Forever*. Because I'm getting married."

"You make it sound like you're off to the gallows."

"I'm not ready for *forever*."

A twinge of panic ripples through me. "You're nervous. It's normal."

"Maybe it is nerves, and maybe it's something else. Whichever, it's sitting here," he taps a finger against his chest, "like an anvil." Shakes his head, tears stand in his eyes. I'm stunned—I haven't seen Dennis cry since we were kids.

"Last night, while watching TV," he says, "I suddenly realized I've been waiting for something to stop the wedding— that we'd run out of money, have no place to live, or my folks would call it off."

"*Hoping* it would be stopped? Why didn't you say something?"

"I don't know."

"But the ceremony's in an hour!"

"Christ, I know, I've set this great big thing in motion, and I'm wondering if I can let it carry me over the edge."

"What?"

"Everything'll be different after today, different forever, and it makes me feel like I'm falling off the edge of the world."

"Holy shit."

"I can't believe I'm saying this," Dennis says, "but I've got to think around this."

He's echoing thoughts I've had for the last year. What am I to say? *Sure, forget about the whole thing.* And once everybody—from the minister to Mira's great grandmother—gets done killing Dennis they will ask what I did to save the wedding.

"Do you understand?" Dennis says. "Have you ever had *forever* staring you in the face?"

"No."

"Same here—until now. I mean, spending my *life* with Mira . . ."

The last of my shock wears away. "What're you saying? Today's an *accident?* You asked her to marry you!"

"It seemed like the thing to do. The next logical step."

"Where's that logic now?"

His face goes blank and I feel awful; my words land more solidly than I intend.

"I'm asking myself that," he says.

Suddenly, I'm wondering where I've been up to now?—this morning, this year? I've thought a thousand times about having a talk with Dennis, over a game of pool, a couple of beers, *So, how are things with Mira? Are you as serious as she seems to be?* But questioning a guy—even your best friend—about the girl he loves is risky. No telling how he will react, because you're not just talking about his girlfriend, or fiancée, you're poking a finger at something fundamental in him. Maybe that's rationalization, maybe it's good sense, but while I waited for the right time and words, a year has slipped by. So, do I tell Dennis what I really think, only to have this spell of nerves pass in a couple of minutes? What would he think of me then, trying to talk him out of the wedding less than an hour before the ceremony?

"You probably think I'm crazy," he says.

"No." I lean against the doorway. "Have you said anything

to Mira?"

"No. It started last night—then hit me about five minutes ago."

"Do you love her?"

"Of course. But I can't help thinking that all I've really wanted right now is to move out on my own."

"Why haven't you?"

"Mira," Dennis says. The sound of her name is like a moan. "If I moved out she'd want me to move in with her, but you know my folks—they'd have a stroke."

"Why not get your own place anyhow? Mira'd never break up with you."

"We'd waste money on *two* places and end up staying at one, anyway. You don't know how Mira is when she's disappointed."

There's no getting away from Mira's *needing*—that's her hook in Dennis. Has been since the start. And once the hook is in a guy, it's all over. You can admit it's there, you can resent it and hate it, but you're powerless to remove it.

"What do we do?" I say. "Want me to go downstairs and tell your folks?"

"No, I gotta think."

"You've had a *year* to think! You should've told Mira."

"I couldn't let her down."

The hook.

"If you called this off weeks ago Mira would've been disappointed. But you'd have the support of me, your parents, everybody. Back out now and they'll want to kill you."

"Even you?"

"Of course not." Why do I feel like this is my fault? "What do we do, then? Go out to my car and drive away? Then what? Leave a note for your folks? For Mira?"

"No."

"Den, doubts aren't terminal. You have to trust yourself. You've always had the choice—stay with her, or leave. You've stayed. So, trust yourself." The words come out so easily I nearly believe them myself.

"I don't even know half of the people coming today. She says that doesn't matter. After reading those damned bridal magazines she's expecting at least a hundred bucks from each couple."

"That's how it goes."

"But *expecting* it, that feels wrong."

"Then let her deal with the cards. She's done everything else."

"That's not the point."

"What is then? You want me to help you bail? Think about your folks, about Mira. Think of the money you've laid-out in deposits for the hall, the photographer, the florist."

"But it—"

"But nothing! You asked her to marry you! Why're you choosing today to grow some balls?"

The words are like a gun blast. I can't believe I've said them—or, can't believe I waited this long. Dennis looks like he's been kicked in the stomach.

"What?"

The expression on his face has played on my mind all these months: tell him the truth and he'll look at me like I'm a stranger, lose his friendship. When he asked me to be his best man I actually considered saying something about Mira, and the hook, and her needing. But I balked. Simple as that. Feared this look of shock, affront, betrayal. Knew he would marry her anyway. My mind translating his question into, *Do I want to keep Dennis as my friend?* So I said yes.

"I'd do anything for you," I say, "but if you're bailing, you're doing it alone."

"What do you have against Mira?"

"Nothing."

"You're a fucking liar!"

"I'm just saying—"

"A fucking liar!"

"Dennis?" It's his mom. I duck my head out the door and see her coming down the hall.

"What?"

"Mira's on the phone," his mom says.

"Right now?" he says, standing. "What's she want?"

"To talk to you," she says, "what do you think?"

The rogue part of my conscience hopes she's calling to back out. I beat the voice down, feeling like a bastard, unable to silence it. I step out of the way, and Dennis goes out to his parents' bedroom to use the telephone. His mother turns to me.

"Is your speech all ready?"

"Yeah."

"How's Dennis doing? He seems tense."

"Just a few jitters."

She smiles. "And when are *you* finally going down the aisle?"

"It's like lightning striking," I say. "You just never know."

Dennis' mom laughs, and straightens my tie. "We should leave in about twenty minutes." Then she heads downstairs.

Watching her go my mind makes a strange crosspatch connection to a memory from a couple of months ago: Dennis and Mira and I went to a movie, some chick-flick. The TV ads indicated it might have been bearable, but the film turned out to be the usual clichéd crap. On the way out, Dennis ducked into the bathroom. As Mira and I made small talk, I said, joking, "You probably gave Dennis a real fight coming to this movie."

"No," she said, "we never argue."

I thought she was kidding.

"What do you mean?" I said.

She frowned. "What do you mean, 'What do you mean?' We never fight."

I picked up on the shorthand of the situation, suddenly feeling like I was coming from a funeral: Dennis had chosen the movie.

Looking at his empty bedroom I wonder just what is my problem with Mira, with their marriage. Far from being the jealous friend, no one was happier than me when they first met. Dennis hasn't had many girlfriends, and he's been third wheel many times, coming out with a girlfriend and me. No doubt he's sat across from me in bars, restaurants wondering what the hell I was doing hanging-out with some of the girls I've dated. Thing is, I didn't propose to any of them. Most of my relationships haven't worked out. I'm going stag to the wedding today. It's not Dennis getting married that bothers me, but the sense that he's settling. And if Mira's always *needing* this early on, she'll only devolve into *demanding*, turning into some cartoonish nagging wife right out of a chauvinist's nightmare.

Dennis returns, and sits on the bed. He looks at me. "What're you saying about me growing some balls?"

"Nothing."

"Bullshit."

I shrug and sigh. "If you had doubts, you should've said something earlier. Do we go downstairs and talk with your folks? That's what we need to do if you're pulling the plug."

He looks at the floor.

I watched him a few moments, then said, "How's Mira?"

"She wanted to hear my voice," he says. "Wondered if I'm as excited as she is."

"What did you say?"

"I'm more excited."

I stare at him. He won't meet my gaze. "I'm being a dick, I know," he says. "You've never given me bad advice—say I should marry Mira and I will."

God help me, I actually consider saying, *Don't do it. I'll help you move your stuff back from the apartment. We'll see about breaking the lease. I'll help you explain this to your parents, to everyone, even Mira if you like, because we're buddies and I can't let you go tumbling into forever if you're not ready.*

But what about days from now, after Dennis has heard from everyone? How will my words hold up after dealing with his parents, returning wedding gifts, or facing Mira? I've seen it right here: doubt rises right out of the air, swallows you whole. My words might be deliverance now, but in a couple of days. . .

I close my eyes. "Marry her, Dennis."

"Marry her," he echoes.

"I'm the easy one," I say. "Do you want to see how it goes with your mother?"

He rises from the bed and goes into the hallway. Part of me hopes he's going downstairs to tell his parents that he's not going through with the wedding. There's no sound of his footsteps on the staircase. A moment later I hear him brushing his teeth in the bathroom.

I approach the bed and look over his speech.

. . . express our thanks to everyone who came from out of town, especially. . .

. . . and my parents who raised me well and taught me every good thing they know. . .

. . . Mira, my bride and my love, I look forward to spending every day from now until forever with you. . .

. . . my best man, who has gone from throwing snowballs

with me in the schoolyard, letting me beat him at pool, to this day, standing by me like he has always stood by me. . .

I gaze out the bedroom window, down at the empty backyard, and recall the games we played as kids: badminton, basketball, strikeout, even lawn darts. For all of our competitions—sweat flowing freely, scores tied at game point—Dennis always played square. That's what made us friends from the beginning.

He comes to the doorway. "Do me a favor?"

"Anything."

"Say nothing to Mira about any of this."

"It's forgotten."

He nods. "We may as well go."

As we walk down the stairs I put my hand on his shoulder.

Grudgingly

The drive back to Windsor was a nightmare: sleet and snow—all the worst February can throw at a traveler. My plans for spending Spring Break with Hanna in Cancun fell through, so I opted for snow-mobiling in Peterborough with my old friend, Tom, who attends Trent University. When Cancun first unraveled, I considered going home to Sudbury for the break—using the occasion to tell my parents that Hanna and I had split up. When I called home, I'd barely said a word when my mother told me about the ski-trip she and Dad had organized with friends for that week. She then asked if Hanna and I were getting excited about Cancun. I winced and said yes. Then I called Tom.

Setting out from Peterborough this morning, I was actually optimistic about the drive. Within an hour, however, a snowstorm blew in faster than forecasted, and traffic slowed to an unsteady crawl. The monotony of the highway was interposed by moments of jangled anxiety, watching impatient motorists dodge snow removal trucks, and swerving around slower moving cars. At one point, traffic stopped altogether. When it finally got going again, ninety minutes later, I glimpsed the accident that had caused the delay—three police cars and a wrecker flanked a mangled Chevette caught between the trailer wheels of a transport truck. The car's roof was crushed, its windows obliterated, and its doors cut away. The flares on the highway shoulder seemed to burn in memorial rather than warning.

And so a seven-hour drive stretched into eleven.

Now, nearly eleven p.m., I'm back at my apartment, worn out, but too keyed-up to sleep. Luckily I've returned a day early. I'll sleep all day tomorrow. Then it's back to classes on Monday.

Kicking off my boots and hanging up my coat, there's only one thing on my mind: beer. There are three in the fridge—a sight as welcome as a St. Bernard rescuing me in a blizzard.

As I flop onto the living room couch, I grab the cordless phone to check my voice mail. A swallow of beer goes jagged in my throat as the computerized voice says, "You have twenty-two messages. To hear messages, press one . . ."

"What the hell?" I mutter to the empty apartment.

I don't get that many calls in a month.

I press number one and listen to messages from friends, acquaintances from school, the English department secretary, professors, even Hanna—all calling for the same reason.

Wondering if I am still alive.

After the final message plays out, I sit staring at the phone.

Is this a joke?

I grab my coat and head outside.

Cursing the cold, I go around to the back of the apartment building where the garbage cans and recycling bins are kept. The storm that slowed my drive must have already passed this way because the sky is cloudless.

With the moon's light reflecting off the snow-covered ground, I can see well enough to search through the recycling bins for yesterday's newspaper. Soon I find one and return to my apartment. There, in the sober glow of my halogen reading lamp, I look over the obituary section of *The Windsor Star*:

DUN, Larry, aged 27 years, student of the University of Windsor, died suddenly on February 22. Funeral arrangements are incomplete. Inquiries call Arsenault Funeral Home 255-9179.

It sure as hell reads as though it's for me.

Was he murdered? Killed in a car accident? Suicide, maybe?

And everybody wondering if it's me.

My surname is common enough, but rarely spelled with one N, as my family spells it. The age listed is five years ahead of mine, but in most of the messages people wondered if that was a misprint.

My mind reels.

Do I call Arsenault Funeral Home? There's probably nobody in at this time of night to answer the telephone. What good would it do anyhow? *I* know I'm not dead.

I read the obituary again, and it all piles up on me: the shock of the telephone messages, dismay seeing *my* name in the obituary; the mangled Chevette slumped at the side of the highway, earlier. All tied together with a superstitious pang.

I dial my parents' number, unable to recall when Mom said they'd be home from their ski-trip. The phone rings three times before the voice mail picks up.

After giving the time and date, I say, "It's just me. There's been some kind of weird mistake down here—an obituary with my name appeared in the newspaper yesterday. I've gotten a bunch of calls about it, and you might, too. Anyhow, I'm fine, it's just some mix-up. Call me when you get in. Bye."

Then I toss the phone to the other end of the couch.

I drink my beer, and in the space of a swallow the silence of the apartment settles on me, as it often has since Hanna left. It's never worse than on rainy Sunday afternoons when I have heaps of homework and no inclination to do it; when there's nothing on television and nobody to call because they've all got their own work; and I lie on the couch listening to the rain tapping against the windows, or looking at the sullen clouds crowding the sky. The silence and boredom mingle together, seething from the walls and ceiling. Suffocating.

Hanna left three months ago. It was an abrupt split, set in motion with "I'm not happy." Amazing how three words can change your life—the shock and suddenness left me guttering. Still, I helped Hanna move. She asked me not to, but I helped anyway. Took us three hours and I don't think her friend, Janice, made eye contact with me as many times that morning. Whenever I picked up a box, Hanna would say, "You don't *have* to do this, you know." But it was easier than sitting in a bar somewhere, torturing myself with images of Hanna and Janice struggling with her dresser, boxes of books, and suitcase. I knew how heavy they were from when we moved into the apartment.

Even with all of her stuff gone, Hanna's still here. I see her curled in the chair by the window, reading—her long hair wrapped in a towel after showering. See the wide wooden sills lined with her plants, which I knocked over every time I opened a window. Still hear her humming as she makes tea in the kitchen. I admired her surety about things; she was never halfway on anything: movies, food, music, people. She always seemed to know what she wanted—and one day decided she didn't want me anymore.

She left me the bed, and this old couch that smells like moldy bread—we bought it for fifty bucks at Value Village. There were no arguments while dividing the things we'd bought together. She took what she wanted. It didn't matter to me. She left me the vacuum cleaner, too.

The quiet of the apartment bears down on me.

I should be making phone calls, but I finish my beer instead.

Then I get up and put on my coat and boots.

* * *

Weary of driving, I go for a walk, mulling my situation.

This might all be funny if everyone hadn't sounded so concerned in their phone messages. My mind circles Hanna, wondering how she reacted to the obituary. I heard the bridled hysteria in her messages. For one second something morbid and malicious in me almost wishes I were dead, and materialized in the apartment Hanna shares with Janice—just to see.

I'm reminded of an episode of *The Twilight Zone*, where a man flips a coin into a newspaper vendor's cash box, and the coin lands on its edge. For the rest of the day the man can read other people's thoughts—and feels isolated, alien with his new ability, unable to tell anyone about it, unable to believe it himself. Finally, after work, he returns to the newspaper vendor and knocks the coin over onto its face, breaking the spell.

And here I am, alone, feeling like a ghost hiding between walls: nobody knows I'm here, but *I* know I'm here.

Downtown Windsor is virtually deserted.

I turn a corner and hear music—or, rather, electronic percussion coming from a club. *Dante's*, the sign above the door proclaims in jagged green and yellow neon. I go inside, needing the distraction of noise and people.

Normally, I hate dance clubs—they're so obnoxiously loud and crowded and dark; altogether too surreal for me when I'm drunk. *Dante's* is no exception. The music blares with enough force to shake the stones loose from the cavern-like walls. Lights flash in blinding strobes. The place is crowded with people dancing, reeling, making-out, picking-up, falling down.

Wouldn't it be great running into a friend who's seen the obituary? Lazarus back from the dead—in *Dante's*. We'd laugh, have a few drinks, then start a rumor that I am alive.

Or, I could be like a movie hero who survives a near-fatal accident, or assassination-attempt, and now has the advantage of taking his enemies totally by surprise. Or, take this chance to change my identity—like Jack Nicholson in *The Passenger*—and live a completely different life. Maybe I'll just cut the obituary out of the newspaper and frame it—a memento along the line of having lightning in a mason jar.

Moving through the crush of people gathered around the bar is like fighting whitewater rapids. Finally, I get a beer and step away from the dance floor, which teems with lolling heads, flailing arms, and bare midriffs. A hand clutches my forearm. I turn to find a pretty pony-tailed brunette smiling at me: blue eyes, slender lovely body, striking.

She leans close. *"Larry!* I thought it was you!"

I squint amid the strobing lights.

"I'm Kelly," she says. "Kelly Hines."

I look at her again—Kelly. We hug. She's my cousin.

"Hey, how's it going?" I say; my words lost to the thrashing music.

Growing up, I had seen Kelly and her three older brothers on birthdays, at Christmas, and Sunday visits. As we got older, the family saw less of each other. Kelly's a year older than me, and came to Windsor a few years ago, enrolled in the university's School of Dramatic Arts. I called her when I came down for school a year later. We double-dated a few times, back when I first met Hanna, then we never got around to calling each other again.

There is a blessed lull in the music and the glut of dancers divides and sub-divides, and crowds toward the bar.

"Are you still at school?" Kelly asks.

"Nearly finished my English degree."

"Impressive."

"Keeps me busy. And yourself?"

"I'm taking a break from school—waitressing, earning some cash so I can make the audition rounds in Toronto."

I finish my beer and order a drink for Kelly.

She leads me to an area twenty feet beyond the dance floor, where there are tables and booths. We take a booth near the rear wall and catch up with one another—leaning across the table, shouting over the music—talking about school, the family, reminiscing about old times.

At the stroke of two, the music stops and the house lights come on. The dance floor clears and the wait staff hurries around clearing tables. To my surprise I actually feel drunk. Kelly is composed, but I'm sure she is drunk, too—she's half my size and had at least five drinks since we sat down.

"I hate these places when the lights're on," she says, and I detect a slur to her words. "Hang on a sec. I left my coat in the DJ's booth."

We head for the door when she returns.

"Didn't you come with anybody?" I ask as we step outside.

"Some girlfriends. They left around the time I found you."

"No boyfriend?"

"Nobody steady."

The wind has picked up outside, and grips us immediately. I slip my hands into my pockets and Kelly clasps hers around my bicep, leaning close. I glance at her hands. I'm grateful for her closeness, but it strikes me as odd. Easy man, I think. You're still singed from Hanna—Kelly's just keeping warm.

"Maybe I'll pass on Toronto and move to California," she says.

The sidewalks are filled with huddled couples and groups coming from clubs and restaurants, hailing the few taxis in the street. "Wanna share a cab?"

"We'll freeze waiting for more," she says. "I don't live far." The slur adds a funky slowness to her speech.

We walk in silence, huddled close, and my thoughts make their familiar drift to Hanna: walking with her arm-in-arm on cold nights, going for coffee after studying. I enjoyed her spontaneity that way—it was never too late to head to the all-night coffee shop around the corner from the apartment. Even after years together, it still felt like a date.

When we finally come to Oak Street my face is frozen into a grimace against the wind. "Come in and warm up," Kelly says, leading me up the steps of a four-unit brownstone. "I'll make coffee."

I follow her to an upper floor unit. Inside, she hangs up our coats and heads into the kitchen. "Make yourself comfy. Hope you don't mind instant coffee?"

A black futon is situated against the far wall. The coffee table is a wooden crate. A bookcase stands opposite the futon, to the side of a television set. On the other side of the TV is a round, overstuffed chair and a reading lamp. I take off my boots and sit on the futon, holding my hands by the radiator under the front windows. As the warmth moves from my hands into my arms, drunkenness seeps through me all over again.

"Shot of Bailey's?" Kelly calls from the kitchen.

"Please."

She enters a few minutes later with two mugs.

"So," she says, curling up beside me, "you haven't mentioned your girlfriend all night. How's she doing?"

I half-wince, half-shrug. "She moved out three months ago."

"What happened?"

The question startles me. I guess I'm just used to my friends, whose idea of drawing me out is plying me with beer and nodding a lot. *What happened?* has been my daily whipping post for the last three months. Then the scene plays through my mind with movie trailer regularity: Rainy Sunday evening, I'm sitting in the living room, studying. Hanna comes out of the bedroom where she had been looking over brochures from the travel agency. I push my books aside, ready for a break, but the grave expression on her face makes me uneasy. She sits on the edge of the couch and says, "Larry, I'm not happy."

"With what?" I say. But I know. The arguments have gotten more frequent in the last half-year, since she left school and started working.

"Have you met somebody else?" I ask, the words falling out of me.

"No, I just need a change," she says. "Everything's gone stale."

And so the plans and promises of three years with Hanna unravel at my feet. I try to reason with her, but that only makes it worse. She cries, says she's sorry, and I sit there like a man at the foot of a mountain, watching the avalanche gather force, unable to run.

"Hanna was tired of living like a student," I hear myself say. "She got a job with a travel agency, and now she wants to travel the world."

"And you don't?" Kelly says.

"I'd love to, but it takes time and money—two things I don't have."

An awkward silence threatens to creep into the air. Kelly offers more coffee.

"Maybe I should go," I say. "I'm keeping you up."

"Not at all." She goes into the kitchen. "I'm off 'til this

evening."

Watching her, a thought rises from the shadows, taking me by surprise: Kelly's beautiful. If I didn't know her, and had just met her at the club tonight, by damn if I wouldn't want to take her home. And already I'm laughing at myself. That's good, Tarzan, I think. Fantasizing about a blood relation. A sure cure for a broken heart—sex that's a shade away from incest.

But there's no getting around it—Kelly's got a wonderful body, bright, thoughtful eyes, and something about the bob of her ponytail is heartstoppingly sexy.

She's not a *blood* relation. The thought comes, random, orphaned, like a rock thrown through a window. Sure enough, I think, recalling my mother once telling me that Kelly had been adopted into the family.

Fuck off with that, already. She's my *cousin*, for God's sake. What's "adopted" got to do with anything? She's family.

But if anything were to happen . . . part of me hints. There'd be nothing, technically, wrong with that.

Kelly returns, and I say, "I had a hell of a drive in from Peterborough today."

She sits next to me, Indian-style, with a knee resting on my thigh. "I heard on the news there was a pretty major accident." She pronounces it *assident*.

My compass arrow must truly be spinning in circles, wondering if Kelly's actually coming onto me. It's one of the worst side effects of the break-up—overanalyzing all my interaction with women. Reading reams of intent and emotion in casual eye contact, whether it's at the library, a bar, or the supermarket—all fueled by the flipside of freewheeling bachelorhood: terror that I'll be alone for the rest of my life.

The moment passes, and I tell Kelly about the mangled Chevette by the side of the highway.

"At least you got back okay," she says, and heads back into the kitchen.

Suddenly recalling the obituary, I say, "Not according to the *Star*."

She returns with the Bailey's. "What's that?"

"My obituary was in yesterday's paper?"

She frowns, asks what I'm talking about. I explain.

"That's creepy," she says, pouring Bailey's into her mug. "Creepy, but kind of cool." She tops up my drink.

"I was thinking the same thing."

"Have you called anybody?"

"Left a message for my folks. I'll call everyone else tomorrow."

"So, I'm the only one who knows you're alive?"

I laugh, surprised. "I guess so."

Kelly's expression turns serious. "Now that I think about it, how do I know you're *not* a ghost? Maybe the obituary's right."

"What?"

"I haven't seen you since grandpa's funeral, then we meet tonight—after your obituary appears."

"Coincidence."

She closes one eye and looks at me. "I think you're a ghost."

"Well, I could be."

"Then whatcha gonna do? 'Cause you can do anything now—fly, walk through walls, spy on people. Maybe I'm the only person who can see you." The slur has deepened her voice, making her words lovely and gravely and elongated.

I lean over and kiss her.

She doesn't resist, but kisses me back. My hands find her breasts, and Kelly wraps her arms around my neck. That ghost-between-the-walls feeling sweeps through me anew, and

I nearly expect to find Hanna in my arms when the kiss ends.

"So, whatcha gonna do, Mr. Ghost?" Kelly drawls.

I think of the addled businessman in that old *Twilight Zone* episode, tortured by his ability to read minds—see Jack Nicholson rummaging through the pockets and luggage of the dead journalist in *The Passenger,* scavenging his new identity. I want to read minds; to come back as someone else. Feels like I'm halfway there, sitting here with Kelly, who's looking at me with an expression shifting between arousal and dismay. I want to undress her, hold her, kiss her, make love to her.

I want her to be Hanna.

As the gyre of my thoughts widens, my fatigue and drunkenness mingle . . . and all I want is to close my eyes.

"If I'm dead I need to lie down," I say.

Kelly lifts my legs onto the futon. "If you fly," she says, her voice very close, "tell me where you go."

"You sure *you're* not dead?"

"How can I be? Cantcha feel my heart beating?"

"Wha—?"

"Be quiet and feel my heart beating," she whispers.

And sure enough she's right—her heart's beating against the side of my ribcage. She's not dead, then. I must be.

Because I can fly, just like Kelly said. Not through the air, or through walls, but through time, back to Hanna, back when we first moved in together and were still giddy with the freedom of it all. Sleeping with her. Waking to find her flopped on the other side of the bed with the sheet and blankets wrapped around her. Some nights she curled around me for warmth; her breath on my neck, her heart beating against my ribcage.

I snap awake to complete darkness, warm after sleeping in my clothes. My left arm tingles, asleep. I can hardly breathe.

Try to get up, but I can't move. Then I hear a moan. A girl's voice.

"Wha—?" I croak.

The moan comes again.

"Hanna?" I whisper.

The weight on top of me shifts and I roll onto the floor, dragging my tingling arm.

"Come back to bed," the voice says.

I crawl across the floor, extend my hands in the dark and feel something cool and slender. A lamp? Feel for its switch, and blind myself turning it on.

"Hey," the voice says. "I'm cold."

Then it hits me. "Jesus Christ." Cousin Kelly. Her name flashes across my mind like a warning flare. I'm at Kelly's apartment. Did I actually kiss her? I try gathering my thoughts, but everything's all over the place: my obituary, Kelly, *Dante's*, Hanna . . .

"I'm cold."

A single thought rises from the clutter: gotta get home. I slip on my coat and step into my boots. I drape Kelly's coat over her, then flick off the light. "I gotta go," I whisper, heading for the door.

I always feel like The Incredible Shrinking Man when I'm hung over, where walking a city block seems like a Himalayan mountain hike. I check my watch: going on five-thirty. My wits slowly rise above the headache pounding the core of my brain, and I suddenly remember kissing Kelly; feeling her breasts, too, for Christ's sake.

Holy shit, sign me up for an encounter group—I'll bring the fondue and Tab Cola.

I belch up beer and Bailey's; wince and wipe my mouth.

So whatcha gonna do, Mr. Ghost? Kelly's voice drawls

through my mind. *Spy on people?*

Did I actually kiss her? I woke with my clothes on, so things mustn't have gone too far.

Gonna spy on somebody?

If a coin landed on its edge for Hanna, I'd want her to know what I had felt after she left—how awful the nights were without her, with the sullen boredom seething through the apartment, coiling around me. For her to know that one night, the week after New Year's, I went driving because I couldn't sleep. As I cruised the vacant streets an answer came with chilling clarity: Kill myself—drive to the middle of the Ambassador Bridge and leap into the night.

I had stopped at the intersection by the bridge's entrance. The light was red. There was little traffic on the streets and I imagined there was even less on the bridge. And I thought about climbing onto the cold railing of the bridge, seeing the river beneath me, the lighted spires of Detroit on the left; huddled, sleeping Windsor on my right. Then I thought of Hanna, her head placid on her pillow, sleeping in the warm dark of Janice's apartment. Thought about my family, friends, and the strangers who would find me in the water.

When traffic light changed to green, I continued down Wyandotte Street, rather than making the turn toward the bridge tollbooths. Back at the apartment I wanted to feel good about my decision, like Jimmy Stewart at the end of *It's a Wonderful Life*; like Lazarus called from his tomb. I searched for a sense of having a second chance, but I only felt like my old deflated self, as I lay across the couch that smelled like moldy bread. And working my way toward drunk that night, I imaged the rum smelling like oils used long ago to prepare bodies for burial.

As I fit the key into my door, I hear the telephone ringing

in the apartment. My hands are cold and clumsy, but I unlock the door, and get to the phone.

It's Hanna. Why should I be surprised? Fortuna reads too much Sidney Sheldon, I'm only hours after kissing Kelly, and Life's never satisfied sticking it to you until it's blown salt into the wound. Of course it's Hanna.

"Larry!"

"Hey Han—"

"I knew it was a mistake! Have you seen—?"

"Yeah, I saw the obit."

"You sound out of breath."

"I just got in."

"From where?"

"Doesn't matter."

"I've been calling and calling! I went to the apartment yesterday afternoon."

"I went up to see Tom."

"I called your parents, but there was no answer, and I thought—"

"Everything's okay—for *this* Larry Dun, at least."

"Larry," she says.

"I'm still here."

"I feel so bad about our vacation—"

"Why didn't you go?"

"I gave the tickets to Janice and her boyfriend."

"Why?"

"I don't know." She sighs. "I feel so stupid." She begins to cry.

"Take it easy."

"You sound angry," she says. "You can't be angry at me for calling! I thought you were *dead!*"

"I'm not angry."

"I want to come over."

"Still don't believe I'm alive?"

"I want to see you."

I belch into the back of my hand, and close my eyes. "The door'll be open."

"I still have my key."

"Even better."

"I'll see you in an hour, then. Is that okay?"

"Fine."

She pauses. I sense she wants to say something more. "Larry?"

"What Hanna?"

The pause runs on, loud in my ear. "I'll see you in a bit."

The shower revives me.

After grabbing a beer from the fridge, I head into the bedroom and take my suit out of the half-empty closet. I haven't worn it since my grandfather's funeral two years ago. I put on my white shirt, and pull on the pants; sweep some lint from the thighs.

Once I knot my tie and put on the jacket, I will do two things.

First, I will raise my beer to the late Larry Dun, twenty-seven year old student of the University of Windsor, and wish him well, wherever he might be.

Then I will go into the living room and lie down on the couch—eyes closed, hands crossed over my chest—until Hanna arrives.

A final thought lingers: I'm not sure what she wants or if she understands that I'm not the same guy she left three months ago. But if Hanna called to me from the door of my tomb, I would heed her voice. I would draw breath and flex my muscles underneath the funeral shrouds—rise and shuffle through the shadows toward her. And as I approached the doorway I would pull the covering away from my face, so she could look at me. And see.

Hadley

It was the summer before high school, and I talked to her on a dare.

I was at the park on the last day of June, playing basketball with my friends on the blacktop court. The sun glared from a cloudless sky, and the hot smell of grass and dandelions rose in the air all around us. It was hard playing in the heat, and after my friend, Darryl, won the game—sinking a fifteen-footer over two defenders—we retreated into the shade of a nearby tree, where we had left our water bottles.

As I downed my blue Gatorade, Darryl nodded in the direction of the playground equipment. A girl was over there pushing two little kids on the swings. He dared me to go and ask her name.

"If she's cross-eyed and snaggle-toothed," I said, "I'll say *you* want a date."

"Go to hell."

At thirteen years of age I didn't know enough, yet, to be shy around girls. I took the dare and crossed the lawn, wondering if the girl was pretty, or if she'd be angry thinking we were playing a joke on her. Looking at her long brown hair, I tried to guess her name: Jenny, Lisa, Karen. She wore a white tank top and faded blue cutoffs, and stood with her back to me. Her legs were long and smooth and tanned.

I stopped about five feet behind her.

"Hey, how're you doing?" I said, suddenly nervous, and unsure why.

The girl didn't answer. Didn't even turn—she just kept pushing the kids on the swings: a boy who looked about five years old and a little girl, with long dark hair, whom I guessed was about three or four.

"Are you new around here?" I said, a little louder.

No response.

The guys were probably laughing their asses off watching me.

The kids on the swings looked in my direction, and the girl turned a moment later, seeming startled to see me. I don't know how long I looked at her, but for a couple of seconds that's all I could do. She was beautiful. Brown hair and hazel eyes, piercingly pretty—the kind of pretty that makes your eyes focus hard and your windpipe sort of close.

"Hi," I wheezed, suddenly needing to clear my throat.

"Hi."

"My name's Wendell," I said.

"I'm Hadley Graham."

"You new around here?"

"I'm down from Guelph looking after my little cousins for the summer."

The way she looked at me was odd. Like she was concentrating on me. I felt kind of embarrassed, but I liked it. The way she talked was different, too. Like her words were dull around the edges.

"Are you deaf?" I said.

Hadley nodded. "I had encephalitis when I was five. When I got better I couldn't hear anymore."

I never heard the word *encephalitis* before.

She smiled. "It's okay, though. I know what you're saying as long as I can see your lips. So, you better mean what you say to me."

I didn't go back to my friends that afternoon.

Hadley's aunt lived on Cyprus Avenue, a fifteen-minute bike ride from my house.

"She'll probably take in boarders soon," Hadley said one afternoon. "There are four bedrooms upstairs and Aunt Maeve might turn half the basement into a studio for herself and half into an apartment for somebody else."

The day was mild, clouds high, swirled across the sky. It was a week after we met, and I had gone there on impulse after seeing Hadley around the park a few more times. I woke that morning thinking of her; the address on Cyprus Avenue she gave me rolling over in my mind. After lunch I was on my bike pedaling east, leaning over the handlebars. I found her sitting on the back porch, watching her cousins, Jamie and Sarah, splashing in their Mr. Turtle swimming pool.

"Why did your aunt move from Guelph?"

"She divorced in May," Hadley said, "and wanted to live some place else. When school finished, Mom sent me down to help."

Hadley loved her cousins, so the summer was more vacation than work. "I spent a lot of time with Aunt Maeve back home," she said. "I'd play with the kids while she painted pictures in the garage. She had a regular studio out there—paints and pastels and her pictures everywhere. When the kids napped, I'd go out and watch her. One time she did this really great picture of an old man in a rowboat, fishing. I watched her make that picture start to finish."

Hadley watched her cousins. "She gave it to me for my birthday. Best present I ever got."

At one point she went inside to pour us some iced tea. I remained on the porch, marveling at how long her cousins could play in their pool. A few minutes later, Hadley returned with our drinks, and a notebook under her arm.

"Can I tell you something?" she asked.

"Sure."

"I like to write," she said. "Poems." She looked at me,

watching for my reaction, I guess. "Would you like to see some?"

"Sure."

She handed me a spiral notebook with a sunrise on the cover.

On the first page, written in big letters:

POEMS
BY
HADLEY GRAHAM

After that page:

Poem About Being Bored
I wish I was doing something fun.

A single poem appeared on each page.

Poem While Standing in the Rain Waiting for the Bus
I wish I was somewhere warm & dry.

On the next page:

Poem for a Broken Heart
Don't cry.

On the next page:

Poem About Things That Scare Me
Big dogs.
Lightning.
Being alone.

On the next page:

Poem About Things That I Like
Summer.
Cats.
Swimming.
Being by myself.

I read the whole book.

Being thirteen, I never knew anybody who wrote anything, let alone a whole book of poems. Hadley watched at me, waiting for my reaction. I told her what I thought: "These are the best poems I've ever read."

"Yeah?"

"Better than anything I read at school. These make sense."

She hugged me.

Things were different with Hadley. Sitting around and doing nothing was fun with her. I guess it would be romantic to say I lost myself in those summer days, but I didn't. It was more like I found a part of myself—a glittering, scintillating part I never knew was there.

Hadley was the first to hold hands.

And there was the night we rode out to the lake. It had rained earlier and the night air was hazy and cool by evening. Reflections of the streetlights shone on the wet roads, and the moon searched for a way through the clouds.

Riding along Old County Road, listening to the song of the crickets, the wet hum of our tires on the pavement, I wondered if Hadley could remember what it was like to hear. I figured she might and thought about describing the sound of the crickets to her; how big the sound was—then realized she wouldn't see my lips in the dark. I thought to tell her later, but the moment had already passed.

Somehow that got me thinking about her poems, delighting in the fact that she would share them with me—feeling a spark of envy that she could write out how she was feeling. After reading the poems I realized I never said anything to anyone outside of saying hello or telling a friend to go to hell. Even with Hadley, I did most of the listening. Yet I had this aching, bursting feeling in my gut, a sense that there was something I wanted to tell her.

I looked at Hadley. She pedaled evenly, watching the road; her hair swept back, waving behind her.

"Hadley," I said.

She didn't turn.

"I know you're leaving at the end of summer." My throat was tight and I was suddenly nervous. "I'm going to miss you bad when you go."

The words hung there amid the sound of the crickets and the hum of the bike tires. Hadley pedaled and watched the road.

As we approached the lake, I wondered if any older kids were already there. Nothing was worse than riding all that way to find a couple of cars parked at the tree line, and the beach full of high school kids, drinking beer, making out; a portable stereo on a picnic table blaring the Top-40 radio station. Nights they were there, we'd continue down the road to a narrow clearing where people launched their fishing boats. It wasn't near as good as the beach, but better than just riding home.

My worries were for nothing: the beach was empty except for the slanted picnic tables, and the barbecue with a dented oil drum beside it.

The air was full of night sounds: the song of the crickets, the lilting call of a loon, squirrels and raccoons running through the bush; the flutter of wings. The air was heavy with the raw, damp odor of the trees and foliage and sand and water; the beach was flat and unmarked like new-fallen snow.

It was dark, and though my eyes adjusted to it I figured Hadley couldn't see my lips. I wondered how we'd talk, and decided it didn't matter. We left our bikes by some trees, and I slung her beach bag—she packed it with towels and two blankets—over my shoulder and took her hand.

Although the older kids went to the late to skinny-dip, I had no plans of doing that with Hadley. But watching her pull off her T-shirt and step out of her cut-offs; seeing her clad in that bathing suit, sure gave me a stir. I cared about her in so many ways I couldn't even keep track of—but seeing her in that one-piece bathing suit made me want to kiss her all over.

The lake was warm. The moon found a way split in the clouds and reflected across the water in a brilliant, narrow track. It was strange night-swimming with Hadley. Whenever I went with my friends the lake was filled with whooping and hollering and laughing. But she and I were quiet, though the silence was not empty. We swam to a raft anchored thirty or forty yards from shore. The moon hung balanced between the receding clouds; the air cool on my ears and cheeks; and the soft regular lapping sounds of our movements in the water. The night sounds mingled into one constant hum.

I climbed onto the raft first—a wooden platform covered with artificial turf atop a dozen oil drums fastened together—and helped Hadley out of the water. We sat on the edge, breathing deep, shivering; looking at the lights dotting the tree line across the lake.

My chest and back and arms felt taut in the chill air. Hadley glimmered like a mermaid in the moonlight. And I thought, *Kiss her*.

Glanced at Hadley. She sat in lovely silence.

Kiss her.

I couldn't. Couldn't bring myself to move.

Kiss her.

"Hadley," I said. She didn't turn. My pulse thrummed. "I want to kiss you."

I touched her shoulder. She turned. All I could do was look at her; my heart was pounding so hard.

She smiled—

—and pushed me off the raft.

As I surfaced, I heard her call, "Race you back!"

She dove into the water.

I caught her ten yards from shore, grabbing her ankle. She shrieked, startled, laughing. I pulled her back and plunged ahead. Hadley lunged on my back. We tumbled beneath the water and as we broke the surface, gasping and laughing, Hadley slid into my arms and pressed her lips to mine.

A strange, wonderful feeling shot through me, tracing the length of my back, exploding warm in my cheeks and ears. I had kissed girls before, but this was different. I had never wanted it so much. Kissing her lips, cheeks, eyes, forehead, chin; stealing glances of her smooth, placid face; long dark eyelashes, wet hair swept back. Held her close, felt the curve of her hips, ass, legs; the swell of her breasts against my chest.

Finally she opened her eyes, smiling: surprised, expectant. And somehow I was thinking about her poems, wishing I had something to share with her. Felt something stirring, words rising. She could probably have read my lips being that close, but I didn't know how to say what needed saying. I kissed her instead.

When we got out of the water, we headed into the shadows of the surrounding trees to towel-off and put on dry clothes. I wished everything wasn't so wet because I would have built a fire. But we did without. Hadley spread a blanket

44

on the sand, folding it so the damp wouldn't soak through. I sat down. She sat between my legs, facing the water. Wrapped the second blanket over my shoulders and my arms around Hadley.

And it was good. Quiet and peaceful. I kissed the top of Hadley's head. She squeezed my arm. Then, without really thinking about it, I started singing. I never did anything like that before; my friends would have thought I was crazy, but it seemed natural enough. I sang something I heard as a kid. My father loved soul music, Sam Cooke, Marvin Gaye and Jackie Wilson. My favorite song was "Ray of Sunshine," by Malcolm Brooks:

I've got a girl
Who loves me all the time.
I've got a lover
Who knows that she's mine.
My girl's true and
My girl's fine.
She fills my heart like
A ray of sunshine.

I never sang to anybody before and it felt strange. Felt good.

Hadley turned to look at me. With her back against me she probably felt the rumble of the words in my chest. I kissed her cheek and turned her face away.

She picks me up
When I'm feeling down.
She's smiling
When I'm wearing a frown.
My girl's sweet and

My girl's fine.
She fills my heart like
A ray of sunshine.

When I finished singing I kissed Hadley. She squeezed my arm.

Then I listened to the night sounds, looked on the lake: the raft resting motionless, tree line surrounding the lake like a dark, uneven wall. The clouds bright against the night sky. The moon slid behind their gauzy veil.

"Hadley," I said. "I love you."

She squeezed my arm.

The day came when Hadley had to leave. I woke that morning, forgetting she was going home. Rolling over, rubbing my eyes, the realization stabbed into me. Gone. By mid-afternoon she would be gone back to Guelph. Being thirteen, unable to drive a car, having no money for train fare, I didn't know when I would see her again.

Leaned up on one elbow, reached over and pushed the curtain back from my window. Gone. Looking at the empty street below, the sunlight slanting through the trees, I felt it in my bones. Gone. Hadley was leaving and all I could do was say goodbye. We had talked about her leaving; after exchanging addresses there wasn't much else to say.

"Why can't you live with your aunt?" I said one day in the park. "You could go to my school—"

"She needs the rooms for boarders," Hadley said. "Besides, I have to go home to my family and friends."

Looked at my clock: nearly nine o'clock. I got up, put on my clothes and went out to my bike. Coasting down the driveway I thought, *This is the last time I'll ride to Hadley's aunt's.* There would be no other nights with Hadley at the lake. With every thrust of my legs, pedaling my bike, pieces of our summer lit in my mind, taking the form of Hadley's poems:

Poem About Walking in the Park with Hadley
I wouldn't want to be anywhere else.

Poem About Night-swimming with Hadley
I wish we never had to come back.

Poem for Hadley
Don't leave.

Between each image the notion, the feeling, the horrid realization of Hadley's leaving pulsed through me like venom: *Gone.*

When I got to Aunt Maeve's, Jamie answered the door.

"Hey, Wendell," he said; his eyes were red and puffy; his voice sounded tired.

"Morning, Jamie," I said, stepping into the house, smelling eggs and bacon and coffee. Through the hallway, I saw Hadley's aunt at the stove cooking breakfast; an apron tied around her plump waist.

"Come in, Wendell," Aunt Maeve said. "Have you eaten, yet?"

Then Hadley came down the hall to me.

"I hope you don't mind—" I began to say and stopped.

Hadley held me. Her face warm against my chest. When she let go I saw her eyes were wide and worried and reddening. I took her hands. "I know."

She nodded. Then led me into the kitchen.

"Not a good day, is it?" Aunt Maeve said.

I shook my head.

* * *

A half-full suitcase lay open on the bed in Hadley's room. I sat next to it, watching her gather clothes, folding them and filling the suitcase. I glanced at the clock on the nightstand next to the bed: a few minutes after ten. Less than four hours. A terrible urgency took hold of me; so long as Hadley was in this house something could be done, a way could be found to make her stay.

We'll call her folks, I thought. *Call them and explain that I, that Aunt Maeve, her cousins need her to stay.* If it were that easy Aunt Maeve would have made that call.

By quarter to eleven Hadley finished packing. Sat next to me; reached over and gripped my hand. Tears stood in her eyes. Rested her head on my shoulder. I put my arm around her. And she cried.

"I don't want to leave," she said.

"I don't want you to," I said even though she wasn't looking at me. Again, that torrent of words beat in my chest, pressed against the back of my eyes. Everything I felt for Hadley gathering inside me. Gone.

She rose from the bed, unzipped a duffel bag sitting next to the door. Turned to me with her book of poems. She opened it to an empty page at the back.

"Write something," she said, handing me the book and a pen.

"A poem?"

"Anything," she said. "Something for me to read on the train."

Gripping the pen, I looked at the empty page.

"I'll take this downstairs." She went out.

I printed at the top of the page.

Hadley:

Thought for a moment:

I am glad that I met you. I had a lot of fun going to the park with you and your cousins.

No! No! No! That wasn't it!

I thought to cross it out, but didn't want to mess up Hadley's book.

I tried again:

I am going to miss you a lot. I will think about the night we went to the lake when I am at school and bored. I hope you think about me when you get back home and maybe tell your friends about the fun we had.

Read it over and felt sick. *Come on*, I thought, *say it*.

My mind thronged with images and words and emotions, but nothing coherent came to the surface. Soon Hadley came back into the room. "Did you write something?"

I signed the message and closed the book. "Tried to," I said, handing it to her.

"Aunt Maeve made iced tea," she said. "We can sit the front porch."

"Sounds good."

I grabbed Hadley's suitcase and brought it downstairs.

"You go outside," she said. "I'll bring out the iced tea."

I sat on the top step, looking at the neighborhood, hearing the sounds of traffic; a lawn mower droning, a radio playing nearby. And I knew there was a whole city around me that didn't care Hadley was leaving.

Hadley's sad about going home, I thought, but she's got it easy. She's going away from the park, the lake, away from everything that would remind her of me. It'll be easy for her to forget.

Hadley came out with the iced tea. She had been crying

again.

"I'm scared about something," she said.

"Of what?"

"When school starts you're going to be around all sorts of girls. . ." She trailed off. "Girls you can take to movies and dances and concerts. . ."

I touched her chin, made sure she was looking at me. "You think I'd prefer other girls just because they can *hear?*"

She nodded.

"Jesus, Hadley, no," I said. "Screw the dances and movies, I want to be with you."

"I don't even know how to dance."

"I went to a few last year, but I'm sure no expert." I took Hadley's hand, and led her to the center of the porch. Put my arms around her and started humming, moving my feet, turning. Hadley moved with me. My mind cast itself back to the soul songs that played over my father's radio, and my humming turned into singing: a Malcolm Brooks song, "Star in the Night:"

> *The moon journeys alone*
> *Searching for a place to lays its head.*
> *And I look to the stars*
> *Thinking of you alone in our bed.*
> *'Cause when things are going wrong*
> *And nothing's feeling right*
> *You are the star*
> *That guides me through the night.*

My voice was no louder than a whisper, but something about the words, the memory of the song made it seem like I was singing full-voice; singing so Hadley could hear my meaning.

A man has a thousand troubles
And no one to help him fight.
A man speaks a thousand truths
And no one thinks he's right.
When things are going wrong
And nothing's feeling right
You are the star
That guides me through the night.

Hadley held me close; felt her breathing on my neck. The thought that came to me at the lake, came once more: if time is ever going to end it could end right now and I sure wouldn't argue.

Two o'clock came.

Aunt Maeve leaned out the front door. "Taxi's on its way."

Hadley and I went into the house. As she said goodbye to her aunt and cousins, I brought her bags onto the porch. Stepping out the door my breath caught in my throat, the sting of emotion seared my eyes. Gone.

A moment later Hadley came out, tearful and silent. We sat on the top step. I traced my finger along her arm; licked my lips, gritted my teeth; felt my emotions crushed into tears and pressing at my eyes. When Hadley looked at me I saw it— compressed into her gaze I saw everything she felt for me. For that moment I understood why I couldn't say how I felt, couldn't write it down in her book.

Against all my wishing the taxi soon pulled in front of the house; the sounds of the neighborhood died away; there was only my breathing, blood pounding, the creak of the stair as Hadley rose from the porch.

"Guess I got to go," she said. I took her bags to the side-walk.

The taxi driver opened the trunk. I placed the bags in. "Do me a favor and help her with them at the station. They're pretty heavy."

"Sure thing," the driver said and got into the taxi.

I turned to Hadley. She was brave; even managed a little smile.

"I'm going to miss you," she said.

"Me too."

"I'll write as soon as I get home," Hadley said.

"I'll be waiting."

She embraced me. "Don't forget me."

"I won't."

Then she got into the taxi. She waved through the window as the driver pulled away. I waved back. Gone. The taxi turned at the corner and the sounds of the neighborhood asserted themselves again. Gone. I turned to get my bike and looked up at the house. The front door opened, Aunt Maeve stepped on the porch. "Wendell," she said. "Would you like to come inside?"

I gripped the handlebars, leaned on the bike, supporting myself. "Thanks," I said. "Thanks, but I . . ." and the words melted away in my throat.

I got on my bike and pedaled up the sidewalk. And when the tears finally came I didn't stop, didn't care, continuing through the city—sweat mingling with tears—all the way to Old County Road and finally to the lake—legs tired, muscles burning; shirt sticking to my back—where the beach was crowded with parents and kids. Rode to the end of the road, to the break in the tree line where people launched their fishing boats. There I sat, catching my breath, wiping at my eyes, wondering what had just happened to me.

Gone.

* * *

School started a few days later.

My friends avoided me, annoyed that I had spent most of the summer with Hadley—I didn't care, I didn't feel like being with anybody. I walked through my first day of high school with little interest; receiving my schedule, having my photograph taken for the yearbook, finding my homeroom. The only relief to the day was finding a letter from Hadley in my mailbox when I got home from school. The letter was brief and affectionate, ending with a poem.

Poem From a Long Ways Away
I miss you.

After reading it half a dozen times, I sat down to write Hadley. There were a number of false starts, tearing sheet after sheet from my tablet of paper, never getting it right, never saying what I wanted to say. I wrote about missing her, how my first day of high school had gone—but it all read like rambling. When I finished I had the grim sense that I missed getting at my point. Put the letter away, planning to rewrite it later.

As the routine of my days blurred into weeks I saw my friends more often: walking to school, eating lunch in the cafeteria, after school. In October my friend, Darryl, and I went out for the freshman boy's basketball team. And Hadley's letters arrived every few weeks with poems, saying she missed me; all written in her round, girlish hand on small sheets of stationery with rainbows slanting over the top corner.

I tried writing back, but the frustration of writing around my point only got worse—felt it every time I picked up a pen. So many evenings I wrote long gushing letters, saying how I loved her, missed her, thought about her all the time, but re-reading them I found they said little, read almost like crazed fan-letters. So I shoved them into my desk drawer planning to would rewrite them later on.

One evening in mid-November I came home from a basketball game to find a letter from Hadley. It read, in part:

I stay up nights thinking about our summer and I wonder if it meant more to me than it did to you. I never told you before that I cried when I read the message you wrote in the back of my book of poems.

It made me feel terrible. I loved you Wendell but you made it sound like we were just pals all summer. Now you won't even write to me. . .

She ended the letter in her usual way.

Poem for Wendell
I wish I knew what your voice sounded like
when you sang to me.

And I actually thought to gather up the letters I had begun and abandoned, mailing them off to her in a grand package, proving I had not forgotten her. Thought to write a new one explaining how I could never get it right; never able to explain my feelings on paper. Sat in my bedroom, stinging, baffled, embarrassed. What had I done? Nothing, and that was Hadley's point. Wondered how things might have been if I had answered Hadley's letters. She would still be in Guelph and I would be here, missing her. Something more than writing had to be done.

I gathered up her letters and my numerous attempts, shoving them into my pockets and headed outside. It was getting darker early by mid-November and the air was cool enough to need a sweatshirt and a jacket. Although my legs were stiff and sore from playing basketball that evening—a game our team had lost by fifteen points—I rode my bike through the evening-dim avenues toward Old County Road. The breeze was cold on my face and ears, turned my bare hands red. My folks were both working late.

Soon found myself at the lake. It was almost eight o'clock and full dark. The beach was empty except for the shadowed forms of the two slanted picnic tables, the cast iron barbecue off to the side with a dented oil drum next to it: the nights for beach parties were two months past.

Leaned my bike against a tree and walked to a picnic table. Sat down, looking on to the lake, at the lights dotting the tree line nearly a mile away; at the raft anchored thirty or forty yards from shore. During my ride I had thought that going to the lake again would fill me with nostalgia, but there was nothing; probably lost in the cold breeze coming, in the unbroken silence of the beach.

I walked to the tree line. It was difficult searching in the dark—cursing myself for not bringing a flashlight—but I finally found what I needed: a rock. Went back to the picnic table, took Hadley's letters from my pocket, and cursed myself again for not planning better before riding all the way out to the lake—I had no string. I wasn't sidetracked for long, wrapping Hadley's letters around that fist-sized rock, along with my half-finished letters, tying them snug with the laces from my shoes. Then I went to the shore and flung it into the lake.

Gone.

Returning to my bike, shoes flopping on my feet, I thought that Hadley might have understood.

Come Out and Play

The November night is bitterly autumn: cold, leaves strewn, scarcely an evening separating day from night. A wind blows off the Detroit River. Clouds sweep across the sky in ribbed strips of cirrus. The stars hold their place, faint and distant, pinpointing the vastness of space above the street-light-glare of the city. The moon, halved and lopsided, is framed between the buildings looming over Woodward Avenue. Scraps of paper cartwheel in the gutter: candy wrappers, sections of newspaper, handbills advertising tonight's concert at the Fox Theater.

It is Saturday night; the sidewalks of Woodward are busy with fast walking, huddled couples, panhandlers, cops walking their beats, parking lot attendants directing traffic with their flashlights topped with glowing orange cones.

The Fox Theater marquee blazes over Woodward:

NOV. 20
W O L F   K E A R N E Y
ONE NITE ONLY

Searchlights across the street slowly revolve, spotting nothing. The parking lots fill with cars. Fans arrive. The lobby of the Fox is busy with the gathering of tickets, selling of T-shirts and programs and drinks, the air is loud with dozens of conversations. The lights are up in the theater. Spotlights glare at the stage, neatly set with a drum kit, keyboards, guitars on stands. Ushers in burgundy blazers check ticket stubs and lead people to their seats from the curtained doorways of the concourse.

Wolf Kearney sits in his dressing room, sipping from a bottle of water. Adjusts his small oval eyeglasses, runs his fingers through his short black hair. The band is outside the door, drinking beer, smoking, laughing. Wolf stares in the air, his dark eyes distracted, half-frowning. He is tired and irritated tonight; restless and not sure why.

"Rock 'n' roll's about ghosts," he once told a young journalist named Sylvia Crawford. "It's about times past, people who're gone. Except they're not gone. They're with you when you're trying to sleep, pacing around an airport, or waiting backstage."

Nearly thirty years of recording and touring stretch before him in an vast streak of unfamiliar faces and voices talking, laughing, bullshitting, pleading: groupies and journalists. There was Janey Angel from boyhood New Jersey; long tequila nights in 1970's Fort Lauderdale; heroin in Hollywood; nights blurred into weeks by cocaine and Long Island iced tea; doors crashing down in the middle of the night: cops, busts, the ordered stillness of a private recovery clinic. Recuperation and a long sober streak of unfamiliar faces and voices talking and laughing and pleading.

Wolf recalls all of it. The faces. Names.

Sylvia.

Five months of 1977 she spent peering into Wolf's dressing rooms, scribbling notes, prowling backstage, hovering at the edges of parties. Sylvia got her interview the first week, but followed the tour across the country. Wolf wondered about her, that girl who appeared backstage and whose smile seemed to be everywhere. *Groupie with a notebook*, he dismissed her. Until, one day toward the end of the tour, she disappeared.

It was crazy. Hundreds of girls came and went backstage during a tour, yet Wolf wondered about Sylvia, missed her. Half a year later, on break in a New York City recording studio, a familiar voice spoke behind Wolf. Sylvia. Her hair was shorter and gone were the hippie beads and tasseled denim vest. She presented him with a book.

"What's this?"

She sat across from him, watching him intently. "An uncorrected proof of my book. It'll be out in a couple of months."

Glanced at the title page: *Wolf's Lair: On Tour with Wolf Kearney.*

Wolf's manager, Sye Parkland, comes into the room: a heavy, frowning man always smoking and sweating. He has represented Wolf since the singer's early twenties. He is a professional handler, not a friend.

"Everything all right?" Sye says with a grunt, taking a pack of cigarettes from the breast pocket of his ratty blazer. He taps out a fresh smoke.

Wolf looks at the fat man, thinks to say something sharp—he hates being disturbed before a show. Instead, he smiles. Sye doesn't know how to respond to a smile. "Just remembering the words to the songs."

Sye grunts again and walks out, lighting the cigarette from the smoldering butt.

Wolf strums the guitar lightly and listens to the gathering din of the audience: like a seashell held to the ear, waves crashing against a bluff, wind rushing through a cornfield. A wind rushing right through Wolf.

The spring of 1978 saw the release of Sylvia's book and Wolf's double-live album *Oblivion Spin*. Spring also brought for Wolf the paralyzing anticlimax and crushing boredom that followed a tour, especially one so successful. He fought off the post-tour depression sleeping all day, sitting-in on the recording sessions of friends' albums; sessions divided by breaks for drinks and drugs. Hanging-out in hotel bars with Jimmy Page, guitar-hunting with Joe Walsh, trading war stories with Tom Waits over drinks in shadowy bars where the famous and the fearless go when they don't want to be recognized; crashing for the night in Stevie Nicks' hotel room.

No sense to how the days and weeks were spent, no schedule; wherever Wolf woke was where his day began. Because he had to be always moving, doing, playing. The moment he stopped, the boredom came clawing after him.

In the midst of the tumult there was Sylvia. After the parties, on days when the shakes made playing the guitar impossible; when recreation became addiction and using became abuse, Sylvia did not cringe away. Wolf was skeptical, thinking she stayed only for another story about another boring casualty of the 1970's rock 'n' roll scene. And though his mind clouded with withdrawal anxiety and his body wracked with tremors and nausea, he was not blind to what he saw in Sylvia: concern, genuine concern and affection. When his mind finally cleared, when his body healed and his vision sharpened, Wolf found he loved Sylvia Crawford.

As the theater lights dim, the audience's clamor swells to a roar, punctuated by screams and whistles. Ushers become solemn silhouettes in the curtained doorways of the concourse. The audience is anxious and applauding; the stage glows like an altar.

Wolf strums a G-chord. The show's promoter ducks his head in the room. "The lights are down."

Wolf is slow rising and wonders over the restless reluctance that's played on his mind most of the day. Walks out of the dressing room, moves to the side of the stage, where a roadie attaches a wireless hook-up to his guitar.

The band takes the stage, the applause escalating as the drummer beats indiscriminately at his kit, the bassist plucks a few low, reverberating notes; the keyboardist places his beer to the side of his expansive instrument. A moment later the drummer calls out the four-count and the bassist and keyboardist head into Wolf's latest single, "Walking the Wire," from his new CD, *Passing Lane*. The music swells—the tempo is a little faster than the album version—as the keyboardist moves through the signature lead that has been playing on the radio around the country for over a month.

Wolf watches them. They are competent, solid, but few bands ever play his music the way he wrote; rarely catching the *soul* of it.

"What's the hold-up?" Sye rasps.

"Just thinking about the words," Wolf says and steps onto the stage.

The applause doubles. People get to their feet, cheering. The whistles come with new frenzy.

Wolf saunters to the center of the stage, feeling oddly caged within the narrow spotlight. He approaches the microphone, closes his eyes and sings in his flat, uneven voice:

I've walked your roads
Writhed on your floors.
I've loved your loves
Kicked in your doors . . .

Photographers stand in the orchestra pit; flashbulbs go off like sparks leaping out of a fire. At the *Passing Lane* release party a journalist said to Wolf, "I don't think your first single is about a lover, or Sylvia, but about your audience."

Wolf had stared hard at the journalist. "You ever think I might've written it about myself?"

. . . loving you has always been
Like walking through fire.
No matter if I stay or go
I'm still walking the wire . . .

The song feels good, nearly like the night he first plucked the chords and heard the whisper of its lyrics. He leads the band through the chord changes a final time, then brings the song to an end.

It's all about ghosts, he thinks, feeling the applause press against him, thinking how Sylvia used to stand at the side of the stage, or in the VIP section, and he would sing to her. *Except, it wouldn't be just to her.* Wolf frowns. *The audience . . . something in it would rear-up like . . . wind in a cornfield . . . demanding . . .*

The first good decision Wolf made after the *Oblivion Spin* tour was entering a recovery clinic. The second good decision was asking Sylvia to be his wife.

Before the applause dies out, Wolf starts strumming "Friday Night in Spring," which will be the second single from *Passing Lane*. As the audience responds, he sings:

I've tumbled through life
Like a roll of the dice.
The dreams I chase
Are a slap in the face
As they pass me by . . .

And now, months after Wolf first recorded the song, it still evokes those Fridays driving his older brother's blue convertible; having the evening off from his job bussing tables at a Chinese restaurant. Taking girlfriends to the pier, speeding along secondary roads, radio playing, and the thrilling free-feeling pulsing through him, igniting emotions that became lyrics he set to chords—comprising his first album, *On the Loose*, released in 1974.

He married Sylvia in 1979; took her to the neighborhood in New Jersey where he grew up. To the pier, along the old secondary roads. Telling her about the dreams he had while staring out at the water, the waves, wind in his face and future murky as spring fog.

> *. . . I never feel more alive*
> *Than when I'm out for a drive*
> *On Friday night.*

Applause fills the theater at the song's end, all those cheers that no longer sound like adulation, approval. Somewhere during the years of touring the tone of the applause had changed. The concerts were wild affairs, and had Wolf told friends or band members the applause had soured, they would have said he was crazy—the cheering, the whistling, the screams were good, that meant people liked what you were doing.

No, it had changed. Sometime during the *Oblivion Spin* tour, when Wolf took to playing hit after hit, never crafting his show as a series of highs and lows. While it was nearly impossible to hear song-requests shouted by the audience, Wolf had done it during the *Oblivion Spin* tour. Playing whatever songs the audience wanted. And over time the shouts became more insistent, frenzied; the applause pleading, demanding, insatiable.

Perspiration rolls down his face. Wolf sips from a cup of water left on the drum riser. Listens to the audience shouting for "Janey Angel," "Stagger," "Letters in a Drawer." He grabs a towel from next to the drum riser and wipes his face, thinking back to earlier in the day, the band drinking and laughing in the hotel lounge, drinking all through dinner—Wolf wondering how they'd sound tonight. And they were surprisingly tight.

And they'll probably be fool enough to think it's the booze, he thinks, finger-picking the intro to "Letters in a Drawer."

As the audience grows still there are sudden outbursts, "*Wolf!*" shattering the mood. Whistles piercing the stillness. It's begun.

I see you on the boulevard
And walking through the park.
I taste your kiss in every drink
And hear your laughter in the dark . . .

Sylvia sensed it, too, particularly when he played the slower songs:

Something happens at a Wolf Kearney show that seems to happen nowhere else in rock 'n' roll, she wrote in *Wolf's Lair*. *A wild something rears-up in the audience. An entity, a genie rises, bit by bit, out of everyone. The fast songs get the crowd on their feet, standing on their seats, climbing the scaffolding supporting the P.A. system at outdoor shows, but strangely enough it's Wolf's ballads that seem to whip his audience into true frenzy. When the mood slows, the lights dim, Wolf stands there playing his battered six-string Gibson, and his audience erupts with screams and howling you would only hear at a revival meeting or an asylum . . . .*

A shrill whistle comes from the balcony. Somewhere on

Wolf's left comes an indiscernible cry.

I have known you my whole life
And remember your smile.
Waiting long, I will always write
Hoping to banish the miles . . .

One night, in Chicago, 1984, Wolf was cornered by an old hippie at a party following a show. The hippie was the sort Wolf saw at concerts and nowhere else in life. His age was difficult to guess; could have been thirty or fifty; hair having no distinguishable color, eyes dark and flashing, disarming, wise. The type who seemed to step out of the air near concert-time, with a ticket in the pocket of his denim jacket, finding his way backstage, to the parties afterward. At the end of the night he would simply disappear in a cloud of marijuana smoke to reappear in another city, at another concert.

This old hippie seized Wolf by the wrist, narrowing his amber gaze, speaking low and hoarse, "I saw the devils all around you. They went leaping out of the crowd like sparks from a fire, screaming in devil-talk, 'Come on, Wolf! Come out and play with us!' You were surrounded by the end of the show."

Wolf stared at him.

"You're purging them," the hippie said. "People come to be freed and the devils come screaming out!" Then he had leaned close. "Thing I wonder is how's it feel when the devils disappear into *you*?"

Wolf said nothing. The hippie stared at him, then nodded, vanishing among the partygoers.

And the songs are played: "On the Loose," "I Hate My Job," "Sunset Song." The band keeps step with Wolf, playing with authority and familiarity. And though the shouts and whistling and requests continue, there comes a moment— nearly ninety minutes after taking the stage—when Wolf unshoulders his guitar, waves to the audience and walks off.

He returns to the dressing room, closes the door, muffling the audience's call for an encore. Sits down and sips from a bottle of water.

Like singing in a windstorm, he thinks. *Playing under a waterfall.*

The band goes back to their dressing room; probably digging into their cooler full of beer. Can't let the buzz falter.

It was during the waiting moments before a concert, in between encores—when Wolf was silent and tense—that Sylvia would say, "Why bother with this? We could move upstate and write. Sell your songs to other bands. Everybody covers your stuff, anyhow."

Wolf might have had an answer for Sylvia Crawford, but looking at Sylvia Kearney one night during the *Hard Time* tour in 1993, he had nothing to say. He loved Sylvia; she placed no demands on him, but was always prodding him to avoid commitments. Had it been Sylvia Crawford, with her beads and ironed hair and spiral notebook, he might have said, "Life's not about getting by; it's about getting *through*."

Sye Parkland steps in the room; the sound of the audience rushes in with him. Cuts it off closing the door. Wolf grabs a towel from a pile on the couch and wipes his face.

"Must be a full moon tonight," Sye says, blowing smoke.

"Half," Wolf says. "I looked before coming in."

Sye drags on his cigarette. "Thinking about not going back out there?"

"Thinking about it."

Sye looks at the floor, his expression neutral. Turns and

goes out, leaving the door open. The audience is frantic. The band waits.

"Go have a beer," Wolf says to the band. "I'll finish up."

He returns to the stage, steps into the narrow spotlight. The audience is on its feet. He approaches the microphone, surveys the crowd.

"This is 'Janey Angel.'"

Eyes closed to the answering applause, he strums his guitar.

My angel's name was Janey,
Lost her wings flying near the sun . . .

That wind in the cornfield, those waves against the bluff begins to rise—the screams and whistles come with new fury: out of the dark, out of the balcony, the walls, the floor, the air. Sparks jumping out of a fire. Flashbulbs flash. A man leaps into the orchestra pit with the photographers, grabbed by security and led away. A woman climbs onto the railing of the balcony, teetering. Someone grabs her around the waist. Her arms flail, she kicks. Burly men in yellow T-shirts marked *SECURITY* make their way toward her.

The aisles on the ground level fill with people moving toward the stage. The orchestra pit fills with men in yellow *SECURITY* shirts.

Janey angel talked to herself
Always wondering if she was sane . . .

The crowd presses against the wall of yellow shirts.

Denver, Colorado. 1993. The *Hard Time* tour.

"I can't sit through it anymore," Sylvia said to Wolf, as they rode in the back of a taxi. He was seeing her to the airport; Sylvia was flying back to New York where negotiations were going on between her agent and a production company interested in making a film based on a book she wrote about student radicals of the 1960's.

"I don't know if your trouble's ego or insanity," Sylvia said. "But to stand up in front of fans who jeer at you, who scream and wail like they're at some medieval rite of exorcism, is just fucking crazy. I can't watch it anymore. Can't be married to somebody who needs that in his life."

And it had been that night, an hour before the show, that Wolf wrote "Letters in a Drawer." Rarely did a song come so easily. Played it that night during the encore. When finally the show was over, he went back to the hotel. Sat with the band in the lounge, ordering his first drink in more than a decade. Did little for him.

Returning to the suite, pacing the room, looking out onto Denver from twenty-three floors up, knowing that things were finished with Sylvia. No blow-up. No insults or accusations. Ultimately, there was no litigation, just a quiet winding-down; a deflating, undramatic sense that the marriage no longer worked.

And the moment had to be marked, acknowledged. Wolf grabbed his duffel bag where he kept his notebooks, pulled out the tattered proof of *Wolf's Lair*. Took the plastic garbage pail from next to the writing desk and a book of hotel matches. Tore the cover from the proof, set it aflame and dropped it in the pail. As it burned Wolf thought to drop the whole proof in, then decided not to. Instead, he picked up his guitar and began strumming again, breathing in the smoke: memory's scent.

Since that night, four years ago, Wolf has gone through

this ritual, in his hotel room, following each show.

The audience approaches the stage; the sound of his guitar fades in the din. As the music is choked off, his thoughts wander from the theater. *Tonight*. The blur of cities, shows and hotels since his divorce from Sylvia is dizzying. *And what of tonight? Go back to the hotel, to the lounge instead of the suite? No way to put it off all night.*

Until the book is done? he wonders, watching men in yellow *SECURITY* shirts battling the gathering mob at the edge of the orchestra pit.

Twenty-two pages remain.

And then? And then? It's done . . .

Janey angel flew away
On wings she had to borrow.
She gave me a kiss
And left me with this
Song of untellable sorrow.

The photographers flee through a door under the stage. The crowd presses against the yellow shirts, shoving them back. The orchestra pit fills with a massive fistfight. Wolf strums his guitar, hearing nothing over the chaos. The promoter stands off to the side of the stage, shouting; his words are swallowed by the tumult. Sye Parkland stands in the shadows, watching, smoking.

A hand drops on Wolf's shoulder. He turns expecting to find a security guard standing behind him, but finds a fan leering over his shoulder. The fan's age is difficult to guess—he could be thirty or fifty. His hair and beard have no distinguishable color, just a sun-bleached shade that hints at sandy-blonde. His eyes are dark and flashing, disarming, wise. He wears a tattered denim vest; a yellow smiley face button is pinned to his frayed collar.

The fan says something. Wolf doesn't catch it. Then a hand presses against his back, shoves him forward, sending Wolf stumbling off the stage. He lands on heads and hands and shoulders; the guitar slams painfully into his chest. His glasses fly off and everything melts into an indistinct blur.

He struggles to raise his head; blinded by hands and faces. The guitar is torn away. Rolls onto his back. Hands carry him away from the stage, from the horrorstruck promoter, from the security guards wading into the chaos.

He's carried away, hands no longer supporting him, but clutching and tearing at his T-shirt, his jeans, the boots are pulled from his feet. Wolf tumbles down from the hands, onto the seats, gasping, ribs aching. He shouts and nothing comes out of his mouth. Sliding down in between the rows, he looks up to watch the faint light above extinguished by a vast blur of unfamiliar faces and voices shouting, pleading.

Continental Divide

The empty Interstate stretches before the car like a used wick. The morning sky is clear and pink, and I'm doing my best to keep from dozing at the wheel. I'm hung over, but conscious. Leo sleeps in the passenger seat.

The morning is cool for August; saw my breath as I carried our bags across the hotel parking lot. It was all Leo could do getting himself to the car. It's a strange part of the country, the Continental Divide: chill, almost numbing as the sun rises, then ninety degrees by the mid-afternoon. Lower my window a little. The cold air feels good.

Hard night last night. We checked into a hotel in downtown Butte, Montana late afternoon, picked up a case of beer to drink while unwinding from the road, watching cable TV in the room. After showering we headed to the lounge for dinner and staggered back sometime after last-call, having run a bar bill that cost more than our room. Other than whitewater rafting in Banff we haven't done much more than go to nightclubs and watch cable TV. Maybe we'll find a casino in North Dakota. We're not much for sightseeing, anyhow. The trip's been about getting away—from our summer jobs, our hometown—for a couple weeks. And it's been a good time; the laughs Leo and I have, the conversation comes so easily in the lounge: parties, proms, girls, concerts we saw together. Good times.

For all our talking at the end of the day, hardly a word passes between us while on the road. It's not a conscious decision; I only became aware of it a couple of days ago. Driving into Idaho, we had been on the road three or four hours and I suddenly realized, *We haven't spoken since starting out this morning*. There's something about the highway that makes me clench-up, turn to the radio, a magazine, watch the scenery roll past. Or pull out the map and decide where to stop for lunch—then silence until we're out of the car. Maybe it's being far from home, though I'm not particularly homesick. We've been gone only two weeks.

The sun crests the horizon with a vicious glare, and my sunglasses and visor offer little relief. I look around at the sandcastle mountains and empty brown expanse of the Continental Divide. Fargo's the goal today, probably another eight hundred miles away. Then the long haul home to Windsor, Ontario.

Having planned this trip since February, working and saving our paychecks through the final weeks of high school and much of July, there are two essential things we are running low on: money and patience for one another.

With the miles between Fargo and here on my mind—and how the map, with its highways circuiting through the flesh-toned patchwork of states, looks like a skinned animal—I'm late swerving around a pothole. The jolt wakes Leo.

"Holy Christ!" he says. It's been days since he shaved and with his bloodshot eyes and hair messed up, he's looking mean this morning.

"How's your head?" I ask.

"Haven't been this hung over since after my birthday." He reclines the seat, covers his face with an arm.

It's hard to say when I first sensed the growing tension between us. If I were guessing I'd say when we pulled into Banff, four days ago. Having been friends since elementary school, we've disagreed, argued over the years, but when it happens while traveling on empty highways, through barren spaces, it gets me feeling more alone than I ever felt in my life.

A few nights ago I dreamed Leo took off in the car, stranding me at a highway rest stop. I woke in a sweat, disoriented. Then, hearing Leo's snoring, I caught my breath, settled down and realized it was only a nightmare. I've had twinges of that dream spiraling through me ever since.

"I can't sleep," Leo says, bringing his seat up to its original position. "I'll snooze when we pull in tonight." He yawns. "Let's switch."

"Wait 'til we stop for lunch."

"I feel like driving now."

Sometimes there is no reasoning with Leo. He makes his demand and dares you to resist. I have seen him grab girlfriends by the hair over disagreements on what movie to see. He's turned road hockey games bloody over arguments about minor penalties. And then there was the nightclub in Vancouver a few nights ago.

We were at a table with a couple of girls we met earlier in the evening—though Leo and I are only eighteen our fake IDs get us past the most scrutinizing doormen. It was getting late, the club was crowded, and the waitress seemed to have disappeared altogether with our drink orders. Half drunk and impatient as ever, Leo lurched to his feet and headed to the bar for another round. While he was gone some guy sat in his chair and started talking to the girls. The girls seemed to know him. I leaned toward him, and said, "My buddy'll be back soon," I shouted over the music roaring from the dance floor. "He's gonna be pissed at you sitting in his chair."

The guy didn't even look at me.

I put my hand on the guy's shoulder and was about to repeat myself when Leo came back, slamming our drinks on the table, spilling them everywhere. In one quick motion he pulled the chair out, sending the guy sprawling to the floor. If Leo had been sober that would have been enough, but he was drunk and he was angry. He gripped the chair by the back with both hands and slammed it down on the guy. Leo hit him a couple of more time before we fled the club.

"Do I have to crawl into your lap now?" Leo says.

I pull over.

Coming from a place so geographically bland as Windsor, Ontario, this trip west has been a revelation. Since geography lessons in third grade I have seen pictures of the vast rolling plains of the Prairies and the Rocky Mountains, snowcapped and majestic. And still, at the first sight of them from the highway, the mountains were beyond anything I had expected. That was nearly a week ago.

As Leo negotiated the road winding higher and higher into the mountains, I had grabbed my camera and shot a roll of film through the windshield. Looking down, beyond the guardrail at the road's edge, was like looking out of an airplane. Heading down the other side, I saw a series of meandering skid marks on the pavement, veering into the concrete guardrail, which was marked with many different colors of car paint. Luckily Leo knew enough to gear-down so we wouldn't burn out the brakes descending the mountain.

"Think that guardrail would keep a car from going over the edge?" I asked.

"I wouldn't want to find out."

The night before last we pulled into Wallace, Idaho, population 1177, according the *WELCOME* sign. More people attended our high school. I was looking through the auto club guidebook, wondering how many more hours it would be before we found a hotel, when we rounded a bend and saw a sprawling Best Western at the side of the highway. The place was an oasis, with a restaurant, lounge, swimming pool and gift shop full granite and fool's gold.

The desk clerk said the hotel had only opened the week before; we were the first occupants of our room. After cleaning up, we headed down to the lounge. It still smelled of new carpet and fresh wood paneling. The place was empty. The woman working the bar seemed glad to have company, as she wiped glasses nobody had likely used yet.

"I'm originally from South Carolina," she said when I had commented on her accent. "I met Barry, my husband, about a year ago. He was working at a golf course, helping his uncle run the pro shop. I was waitressing at the nineteenth hole."

"What brought you here?" Leo asked.

"The logging company had openings. Barry's from out here and been putting his name in with the forest company for two years. He finally got the call. Barry came out here first. We wrote to each other for about eight months, then he sent for me. We got married two months ago. Good timing for me to get the job here."

"How long did he work at the pro shop?" I asked.

"Five weeks."

"He must've been a hell of a letter-writer," I said.

She nodded, said he wrote fairly regular, and kept wiping the glasses.

With sections of North America so crowded, it's difficult to grasp the emptiness of this region. Staring out the window I think about that woman working the bar at the Best Western. She knew Barry, face to face, not even two months, then moved across the country to marry him after eight months of letter writing. He's out in the woods all day and there she is wiping glasses, listening to cars pass on the highway. Somehow this brings to mind my dream from the other night: coming out of the rest stop bathroom, seeing an empty space where the car was parked minutes before. First thinking it was stolen, but seeing no sign of Leo, I realize he's taken off.

I switch on the radio. Nothing much to listen to: country/western station, a call-in show talking about some murder case in California, a station playing '80's techno-pop. I settle for the country station, listening to a lonesome singer drawling about his guitar being better company than his woman. I sit back, look out the window—

—and see something at the side of the highway.

"Look at that."

"A backpack," Leo says.

It's dark blue with fluorescent green and red trim. The colors stand out like a beacon against the stark brown landscape. It's like the sport duffel I've been using for a travel bag.

"Well, who the hell would that belong to?" I say. "Where's the owner?"

"What're you talking about?"

As we pass the bag, I turn in my seat. *Who would leave it just sitting there?*

We round a bend, and the backpack disappears behind a hill.

"Shouldn't we stop?" I say.

"Why? Probably no money in it."

"Who would just leave their bag there?"

"Who cares?"

"Well, maybe a hitchhiker got hit by a car and rolled down the incline?"

"And his bag landed nice and neat on the shoulder?" Leo says. "Nobody got hit by a car back there."

"How do you know?"

"No skid marks, for one thing."

"We gotta go back."

Leo shakes his head. "We're not turning around."

The dare, waving in his voice like a red cape.

When it comes to disagreements over hotels, restaurants, or who drives the car, I'm willing to compromise. We have been friends a long time.

"Turn back!"

"It's just a fucking *bag*."

I say nothing, as I unfasten my seatbelt. Blood pounds in my temples. We have to stop. I slide over and jam my foot on the brake pedal—a terrible idea at seventy miles per hour.

The tires screech. I'm thrown against the dashboard. My neck jerks painfully, as my head strikes the windshield. The car veers toward the highway's gravel shoulder. Beyond the guardrail is the edge of a twenty- or thirty-foot incline.

Leo furiously works the wheel trying to keep us on the road. The car spins nearly one hundred and eighty degrees. We come to a stop in the middle of the road, facing the way we have just come.

Leo throws open his door. I shift around in my seat and lean back. Close my eyes. My door opens and Leo pulls me out by the collar of my shirt. The left side of my neck screams with pain. There's a dull thudding headache resonating from the core of my head. I shove Leo's hand away.

"What the fuck are you doing?!" he rages. "You nearly *rolled* us!"

I step away from the car. Head rush. Clench my eyes shut. I walk down the highway in the direction of Fargo, until the head rush passes.

He grabs my shoulder. I turn, look at him; I always forget that we are the same size. "Two minutes," I say. "That's all it'd take to check around that backpack—"

"What the fuck *for?*"

"There's nothing out here. If somebody's hurt, who's going to help?"

I head back to my car. Leo doesn't move. He could stop

me, but I know that it means more when he intimidates people into doing what he wants. I get behind the steering wheel; the key is still in the ignition. Thank God. I look up: Leo's glare loses nothing in the rear view mirror.

"You getting in?" I call through the window.

Leo doesn't move.

I start the engine. "Are you getting in the car?"

He says nothing.

I put the car in gear and head back down the road.

The radio is still on: some lonesome lady singer drawls about a honky-tonk jukebox that's better company than her man. By the end of the song I steer around the final bend in the road. Looking over the gravel shoulder for the backpack, I can't help speaking the obvious: "It's gone."

I was right, Leo sneers in my mind. *Who the hell cares about it, anyhow?*

"Where the hell did it go?" I mutter to myself. "No cars have gone by in either direction."

I cross the two-lane highway, pull onto the shoulder where we had seen the bag. I get out and go to the guardrail; beyond is a grade of about twenty or thirty feet to the flat brown expanse. Gazing at the horizon, at the mountains and huge sky above me, I feel smaller than I ever have in my life.

"Where the hell . . . ?"

As I turn to look across the highway, at the mountains barricading the northern horizon, I catch movement from the corner of my eye. Turning back, I see a man on the brown expanse at the foot of the grade, partially obscured by the slope where there's a bend in the road. He's rummaging through the backpack. There's something jarring about seeing another person out here.

Curiosity, instinct—I don't know—takes over and I jump the guardrail, stumble down the rocky grade. The man has his back to me. He wears ragged, colorless clothes. Probably a hobo. He gives no indication that he knows I'm coming until I'm about five yards away. He spins around, wearing the same guarded expression of a mutt that's been caught eating out of an overturned garbage can. Startled. Wary.

We stand, blinking at one another.

From the look of his hair and beard, leathery face, flopped formless hat, to his wild eyes, he is a vision of stark dusty brown. His age is hard to guess. He is hunched like an old man, but there is something about his hands and face that says he's probably no older than forty.

"Whose bag is that?" I ask.

"Mine!" the hobo says, his voice raspy, weary.

My head pounds. Neck throbs. All my fatigue, hangover, confusion over the backpack, funnel into one emotion. Anger. I think of Leo and how there are actually times where I envy him, and his ability to grab a chair right out from under a guy and beat him with it.

"You're full of shit."

"It's mine," the hobo says. He's scared. If he runs I can catch him. Where's he going to run, anyhow?

It's not yours, I think to say, but Leo never wastes words on strangers—

I knock the hobo to the ground: two lunging steps at him, his eyes widen, he raises a protective hand. Too late. I drive my two fists into his chest. He sprawls on the brown earth. I pull the backpack away from him.

"Whatta you doing?" he cries. "That's mine!"

"The hell it is!"

He gets to his feet, sneering.

"Start walking," I say.

He scowls. The bitterness and desolation in his eyes makes me uneasy. It suddenly occurs to me that he might be carrying a gun, a knife. I shouldn't have been so quick to knock him down. I'm dead if he has a weapon.

He hobbles away. My anger curdles. I watch him walk until he disappears around the sloping grade, where there is a bend in the highway.

"Shoulda just gave it to me," I say, kneeling down, unzipping the bag and dumping out its contents.

The backpack is crammed with clothing: socks, jeans, T-shirts, bras and panties. I find no wallet, no ID, only an envelope postmarked three days ago, addressed to Judy Baron of Helena, Montana.

I read it. A long letter, rambling and confused at times, full of *I can't live without you . . . I won't let you live without me . . . .* Signed, *I can't let you leave, Marshall.*

Looks like Marshall came and got Judy, the voice of Leo whispers in my mind.

"But why leave her *backpack* out here?"

Who knows?

Get to my feet, look around at the quiet wide-openness, suddenly wondering about the car. Might have damaged it, slamming the brakes like I did. And wondering, too, if maybe the hobo doubled back, climbed the incline and let the air out of all the tires. I feel my pocket. No keys—left them in the ignition. He might have doubled back and stolen the car. Christ.

Head pounding, thinking of Judy Baron, I suddenly want to be home, back where there are trees and people. Where someone hears a call for help.

I climb up to the guardrail, and toss the bag over—

Leo is standing there, arms folded, leaning against the car. "So, you got it."

"Some hobo was going through it," I say, and tell him about the letter.

He nods. "You might've just left the bum alone, too."

I open the car door. "Long walk?"

Leo throws me to the ground, and stands over me. I shield my face expecting a kick. "You nearly *killed* us for a fucking love letter and some dirty clothes?"

I get to my feet. He moves to grab the front of my shirt, and I knock his hand away. Leo tries again, and I tackle him against the side of the car. The breath rushes out of him. *Hit him,* part of me urges. I clench my fist—for all the mean words, the bullying and tantrums.

But I walk away, rubbing the side of my neck. "I'll fight you," I say. "I'll make you hurt me. And then what?"

"Fuck you."

"Fuck all of this," I say. "We're going to the next town to find a sheriff."

"Whatever you say, cap'n."

We drive in silence to the town of Three Forks.

The road from the highway cuts through the center of town. Across the street from a church and a park is a two-story brick building with a sign out front that reads *COUNTY COURTHOUSE.* I park the car and head inside, not caring if Leo follows me.

The clock in the lobby says it's nearly eight-thirty. The building is quiet; most of the offices probably open around nine or ten. After looking over the directory in the lobby, I head down a hall to a door next to a wall full of *WANTED-*posters. I hear Leo's shuffling footsteps behind me.

The word *SHERIFF* is printed on the door. No sound of activity beyond. I've got an image in my mind that the sheriff's a white-haired man, grandfatherly, possibly wise and interested in the backpack and the letter, and Judy Baron. Another part of me fears I'll open the door and find a dullard shining his badge or standing in front of the mirror in the bathroom, twirling his gun.

The sheriff we find, however, looks like a marine from a low budget war film: wide shoulders, close-cropped hair, stony expression. His response to us, the backpack, is decidedly anti-climactic. Sets it on his desk, glances briefly at the letter, then dismisses Leo and I, telling us to drive safely. Doesn't even ask for our names. Outside the office Leo says, "I guess that's that." No challenge in his voice, no sarcasm.

We start for the doors.

"I gotta piss," Leo says, and turns down an intersecting hallway.

Again, I notice the wall filled with *WANTED*-posters. Looking them over, I wonder if the sheriff will do anything about the backpack.

I feel the stirrings of doubt. Maybe I overreacted. Leo dismissed the backpack as junk and the sheriff showed no concern. If I went back into the office I'd probably find him reading the morning newspaper.

The backpack could have fallen from the roof rack of a car and tumbled to the side of the road. Maybe Judy was traveling with friends, away from a possessive boyfriend, didn't notice her backpack missing until the next rest stop. It could have been stolen from a bus station or a roadside restaurant. Judy might have left it for a moment to use a pay phone, turned and it was gone; the bag ultimately thrown to the side of the road once the thief found her wallet.

Anything could've happened.

Looking over these *WANTED*-posters, pictures of sneering, bearded men; wild-eyed, scars straddling noses, slanting across foreheads and along cheeks. So many faces with names that sound like grunts, hisses: Chuck . . . Wes . . . Dexter . . . Orville . . . . Men wanted for robbery, assault, rape, murder; each of these faces no doubt haunts innumerable victims. Somewhere among the mountains, along the highways, roaming towns and cities, these men are still at large.

Staring into the vacant eyes of the photographs another thought occurs to me: I didn't look down the incline on the *other* side of the highway. Judy Baron could have been there the whole time, lying in the dirt, beaten and bleeding, or dead. Maybe she wasn't there at all. I didn't check—

Leo claps me on the shoulder. I swallow a startled yell.

"We've got some shit to talk over," Leo says.

"I guess so."

Suddenly I'm very tired. I hand him the car keys.

Fargo, North Dakota.

We pull into a hotel around eight p.m.—it's been the longest day of driving yet. The shower rouses me, adding a couple of hours to the night. Leo and I haven't had our talk yet and probably won't until we get back to Windsor. Just as well. We head down to the restaurant for a steak, and we actually converse over dinner. Nothing serious, just one of our usual conversations about girls, memorable parties. Old times. Sometimes I wonder if maybe the past is the only thing Leo and I have in common anymore.

The waitress clears the table and leaves with our drink and dessert orders. Leo gets up from the table. "I'll make a quick call home."

He walks away and a thought crosses my mind: It's strange to be calling now. We did pull in later than usual, but there wouldn't be any harm in calling after dessert, from our room.

For some reason I check my pocket for the car keys—I don't have them. Probably in the room. Then comes an image of Leo pocketing the keys while I was in the shower. Pieces of my dream from the other night flash: coming out of the rest stop washroom and finding Leo, the car, gone.

What the hell am I thinking?

With no conscious prompting the *WANTED*-posters fan out in my mind. Beyond the windows this restaurant, beyond the lighted streets of Fargo, in the shadows past the guardrails of the highways, these men roam, lurk; pillaging stalled cars abandoned at the side of the road, robbing desolate farmhouses of few canned goods and preserves, stalking weary hitchhikers. And I think of the hush of the barren stillness of the highway, of the Continental Divide. All it would take is for a tire to blow out, the engine to overheat, a belt to snap, fuel to run low.

For the car to stop.

Then for the dust-brown hobos would all but rise out of the ground and knock on the windows, begging for money. Or a drifter with murder in his past and a gun tucked in the back of his belt to come along the highway and see the car, see two young travelers staring at the steaming engine—a slow, crooked grin spreading across the drifter's tanned face. And I think of the sheriff of Three Forks and his maddening complacency. Hardly reacted to Judy Baron's backpack, to the letter. Maybe he knows something that I don't. Maybe he understands this sense of inevitability, that it's only a matter of time before the car stops on the highway, and all that wide-open space simply crushes down on a person.

A bolt of anxiety shoots through me.

The car. My keys. Leo.

Where the hell is he? Maybe I should see if he is making his telephone call. If he is, I'll say hello to his folks. If he's not—?

He could be in the washroom. Or down in the car this very moment.

I close my eyes and see those *WANTED*-posters.

As I place my napkin on the table, ready to get up, Leo returns.

The waitress comes with our desserts and fresh drinks. Leo raises his glass. Seems about to say something, but changes his mind. He clinks his glass against mine.

"No matter what," I say, "we're still friends, right?"

Leo looks at me.

"We're friends, right?" I say. "We disagree sometimes, but we're still friends."

"Sure," he says. "Best buddies."

Under the Bridge

It had been a long night, indeed: beers, band practice, argument, and a few more beers. The band agreed on nothing. Money was always the problem: where to get it, how to spend it. Our gigs around Windsor covered the PA and soundboard rentals, and some of the beer for the night—most bars didn't offer free beer to bands, so we either ran a tab, or smuggled in our own. Then, about three months ago, we began recording a CD—each bandmember kicking in whatever cash we could spare to cover the cost. The guys all had side-jobs, and rented a house together. The place was a four-walled wreck, but it had room enough for us to practice; and the neighbors didn't seem to mind. I was in my last year at the university, spinning my wheels through a degree in history. Had my own place across town, needing the room and quiet to study. No matter how we spent our days—working or studying—we spent our nights as the Celtic rock band, Auld Sod.

It was going on three a.m. as I drove down Sandwich Street, heading home, thinking, *Nearly set to press the CDs and Sean wants to tour. Hardly enough money for more T-shirts, and he wants to go back to Boston.*

"We're a *live* band," Sean had said, earlier. "They loved us in Boston last year."

"But St. Paddy's Day has come and gone," I had said. "And it took months to pay off that trip."

"We never got that kind of exposure, *any*where," Sean said.

"The CD will do that, too," Bruce, the band's accordion player, had said. "The band T-shirts all sold, and when the CDs finished, it'll only cost a few of bucks more. And we can send it out to radio stations."

"Randy's bled us for six hundred bucks," Sean said. "Hasn't answered his phone in two weeks. Who cares if Bruce is right, and Randy's on vacation? We gotta cut our losses *now.*"

Bruce knew a guy at the auto plant, who had a makeshift recording studio in his basement. The guy—Randy Kurzuk, a full-time autoworker and part-time music producer—charged plenty, but knew shit-all about recording. Whole sessions were wasted doing sound checks, re-recording tracks he accidentally erased. It was a bad situation, but Randy was half as expensive as the single professional recording studio in town. Our master tape was almost finished, only the mix lay ahead before sending the DAT to be pressed into CDs. The only trouble was contacting Randy.

"*If* we finish the mix," Sean had said, "pressing the CDs is gonna cost another couple thousand." He shook his head. "Randy's fucked us. We should sue the bastard, not give him more money."

The other guys had been silent. They were excited about the CD, I knew, but reluctant to argue with Sean.

I pushed the argument from my mind. I'd talk to Sean, alone, tomorrow.

A final twinge of exasperation twisted through me, as the traffic light at the intersection beneath the Ambassador Bridge turned red. I slowed, looking around. Considered running the light. But with my luck a cop might have been cruising by. I stopped.

As the lights facing the opposite way turned yellow, I eased off the brake. As I was about to stomp the accelerator something struck the pavement in front of my car with a tinny *thunk.*

"What the fuck?"

I got out, looked around the front of the car.

What the hell was that?

Looked up at the bridge. Glanced toward the curb. Nothing.

Bent down, and saw it under my car—a dented Vernor's can.

"Well, holy shit," I said; the can would have gouged the hell out of my car's hood. *Some littering asshole.* I reached under the car for the can, and was surprised by its weight. Seemed full, though it was open and nothing was leaking out.

I got into the car, looked over the can.

A piece of plastic protruded from the can's mouth hole. I tugged on it and a small plastic baggie came out—filled with white powder.

Heard a car approaching; saw the headlights in the rear-view mirror.

I tossed the can and baggie onto the passenger seat, and put the car in gear. Hung a right at the corner—rather than heading through the intersection, and continuing home.

Headed back to the house.

The front door was open—the keys were lost so often it was easier to leave it unlocked. The main floor was dark. Headed through the kitchen and down the stairs to the dank basement. To Sean's room.

"Sean," I whispered. "You still awake?"

His bedroom door opened. "What's up?" Sean worked for a roofing company, and somehow balanced his break-of-dawn start time with band practice.

I held out the Vernor's can, explained how I found it. We stepped into his bedroom; he sat on the bed, I took his desk chair, watching him pull a plastic pouch from the can. Looked at it, then at me.

"Is this coke?" he said.

"I'd guess it's not table salt."

"And it *fell* from the bridge?"

"Scared the shit out of me."

"Was there anybody hanging around?" he said. I didn't understand his urgency. "Somebody might've been waiting for the drop!"

My mouth went dry. "I didn't think—"

"Did you see anybody?"

"No."

"Jesus. You know, I took a law class in high school and remember a Customs inspector coming in. He told us how the Detroit-Windsor border was one of the busiest in North America. Had stories of people stuffing dope into tennis balls, cosmetic bags—soda cans, too, I guess—and throwing them off the bridge before reaching Customs."

"Holy Christ—"

"Anybody who's gonna do that would have somebody waiting below. Were you followed?"

"No."

We went up stairs. The street beyond the front window was empty.

"Maybe I should put it back," I said.

"And what if the drop-guy is still there looking for it?"

"Shit."

Sean examined the plastic pouch in his hand. "The can's *stuffed* with this shit," he said. "It's gotta be worth a few thousand bucks."

I cringed. *People get killed for a lot less,* I thought.

"But you didn't see anybody."

"Nobody." I got out of the car and looked around.

"They probably took a chance nobody'd be around at this hour. Zip around and get it themselves after clearing Customs.

Wonder how long it would've taken them to find the can if you hadn't come along."

"It landed in the middle of the intersection."

"But they couldn't know that from up on the bridge."

A car approached out front. My breath caught; ears bristling, listening for it to stop, for a door to open and shut; the sound of steps on the creaky porch. A rap at the front door.

Sean looked up. The car passed.

"A few thousand bucks," he said. "Listen. We've never bothered with this shit, but think what it's worth. Should we go to the cops? *We* know you didn't do anything wrong, but how long before *they* believe that? Do we flush it? Maybe, but this is a chunk of change." His words hung in the air. "We could use some cash about now."

"You're kidding," I said. "*Sell* the dope? Are you nuts? Do you know what kind of risk you're talking about?"

"All kinds of risks in life."

"What about jail-time? Or dealing with the guys who own that shit?"

"Well, Jesus Christ," Sean said. "Why did you get out of the car?"

"I was startled . . . wasn't thinking."

"When you saw it was only a can, why didn't you drive home? Why pick it up and why bring it here?"

"To . . . talk."

"And I've talked."

And I wondered, too, what brought me back. Reflex. We had been friends for years, since first-year on campus. Anyway, what would I do with the dope at my place? Flushed it? No. Sean was right, it was *crammed* with those pouches . . . Might be worth hundreds, maybe thousands of dollars . . . It was late . . . Startled by it falling so close . . .

Had to think fast with that car approaching.

"We could use some cash," I said, "but if we do this, when do we start robbing convenience stores? What if somebody OD's on that shit?"

I couldn't read Sean's expression. "No argument, but listen: We sell the dope to one person—somebody safe—and we walk away with the cash?"

"Who?"

"Randy."

Randy smoked dope; in fact, during most of our recording sessions, possibly accounting for all his reckless mistakes. He was in his forties and portrayed himself as an original hippie, with his patchy gray beard and stringy ponytail. He worked with Bruce him at the auto plant. Randy smuggled booze and cigarettes in from the States; sold them to guys at the plant. We had bought a couple of bottles from him; figured that's how he financed his recording equipment.

"I can't play," Randy once said, "but I know music. I saw Hendrix and the Doors in Detroit in 1968. Hung-out with Iggy in Ann Arbor. I can't play, but I know what good music is."

I had no contact with Randy, aside from recording in his basement. Had no idea if he was "safe." From everything I'd heard, Sean was probably right: Randy had the interest and ability to sell drugs.

"Your hands won't get dirty," Sean said. "You found the stuff, your part is done. I'll take care of the rest."

I considered this. It was wrong, but there are *degrees* of wrong.

And we needed the cash.

"We'll do it," I said. "And get the master tape, and walk away."

"If all goes well, we'll never see that tub of shit again."

*   *   *

Sean called a few days later, said he contacted Randy—Bruce had been right: Randy was in the States, taking vacation time.

"Listen," Sean said, as I drove us to Randy's house. "He's safe, and very careful. Remember Bruce saying how the cops raided the employees' lockers at the plant, looking for smuggled booze and smokes?"

"Sure, it was in the newspaper."

"Bruce heard the cops were looking to nail Randy, specifically."

"But he came away clean."

"Exactly—because he's careful. He told me how he wants this done. First, no mention of dope. He thinks the cops've bugged his house. No shit. Who knows?

"Second, we're going under the pretence of finishing the master tape. Once we're done recording, I'll ask Randy about buying his truck—" Randy's pick-up, parked out front, had had a faded *FOR SALE* sign in the window for nearly a year. "—You stay in the basement, putting the guitars away. When he and I go outside, you stash the can in an amp. Randy'll test the shit, and call us with a price."

"Stash it in an amp? Why?"

"I'm just going by what he told me to do. Maybe he's worried the cops could come crashing through the door at anytime."

"And we're just leaving the can there? You've always said he's crook."

"He has to test the shit. Won't give us any cash until he knows what it's worth. You want to hang around all day while he does that? Sure, he's been a cock, but he's gonna make a lot cash off this—"

"He'll make even more if he keeps it and cuts out us. What

do we do, then? Call the cops?"

"You wanna call this off?"

I watched the road. Took my time answering. "No."

Guitar cases in hand, we knocked on Randy's door. Took a few more raps before he peered through a window by the door. Sean reached into his pocket and fanned out three twenties and four ten-dollar bills in front of the window—probably from our T-shirt fund. "We need to finish the DAT," he said.

That pissed me off: Sean said nothing about giving him money. Before I could say anything, Randy opened the door. Sean handed him the cash.

"Christ, guys," Randy said. "I'm on my way out."

"We have to finish the DAT," Sean said, stepping in the house.

"I told you never to come without calling first," Randy said. "I got people to see."

"All we need's an hour," Sean said. "Then we're gone."

Randy pocketed the money. His hands trembled. "One hour."

We headed downstairs and unpacked our guitars. Randy sat at his console, stationed on an old office desk. After a quick sound check he waved a shaky hand, signaling he was ready. I strummed the chords to an instrumental we recorded weeks ago, and had been erased. Eight beats later Sean played the lead. Anxious and preoccupied as I was, the session was good. I don't know how Sean managed it, but he played as though music was the only thing on his mind. As I strummed I glanced around the cluttered basement. Didn't miss a beat, but my heart began to race—once they went outside it was up to me; I'd be the last to handle the dope.

Randy played back the tape after the first take. Sounded

good; it was tight.

"Iggy and the Stooges ever do a first take like that," Sean said.

Randy grunted.

"I was wondering about the pick-up," Sean said. "We'll be touring soon, and we'll need something to handle all of our equipment."

Randy shook his head. "I had a call the other day. Guy sounded really interested."

"What'd he offer?"

"I won't take less than eight hundred," Randy said. They went upstairs.

Randy stopped halfway up the stairs. "Pull the front door tight after you," he said.

"Sure."

When their footsteps moved above, I took the can from Sean's case.

In the back of an amp.

There were two small amps on either side of Randy's desk, acting as monitors. The opening in the backs was about two inches wide. Couldn't fit the can through. It would have taken a star head screwdriver to take the back off an amp. I looked over Randy's cluttered desk. Nothing I could use. I guess I had to find another place.

Pulled open the top drawer. Lifted papers and music magazines—and stopped.

There was a gun in the drawer.

I had never seen one outside of films, or television. Knew nothing about them; had no idea what kind it was, though I was certain it was real. Shut the drawer. I opened the one below it, and placed the can under some papers. Then hurried up the stairs with the guitar cases. At the top of the stairs I stopped, put the cases aside. Went back down to the desk, ejected our master tape, and slipped it into my jacket pocket.

Randy and Sean sat in the truck. Randy was trying to start the engine, but it wouldn't catch. I put the guitar cases in the hatchback of my car.

"I'll talk to the guys," Sean said, getting out of the truck. "They know we need something. We'll probably take it."

"Whatever you say," Randy said. "And listen, give me a fucking call before you drop in next time."

The moment I rounded the corner of Randy's street, Sean asked how it went.

"Are you fucking *retarded?"* he shouted, after I told him I'd left the can in the desk drawer. "He said how he wanted it done. There *must've* been a screwdriver!"

"There was nothing! I didn't know what to do!"

Sean slumped in his seat, resting his elbow in the open window, cupping his head in his hand. "Pull over when you see a pay phone. I'll and try and tell him where it is without blowing the goddamned deal."

After Sean made his call we headed to the house.

"Said he'd need a couple hours to test the shit," Sean said.

The place was empty. There was no use hanging around staring at each other, so we headed to the Dominion House. Chris, the bartender, talked with us between pouring drinks, asking how our CD was going. As the time passed I felt something close to relief, glad to be rid of that goddamned soda can—didn't really care if Randy cut us out. We had the DAT. And when Sean got up to make the call, two hours after we first entered the Dominion House, my conscience was actually starting to quiet.

Sean returned. "We gotta go," he said, looking gutted with shock.

We went out to the car. "We've got trouble," he said.

"What?"

"Randy left a message on the voicemail. Said if we want to live through the night we better get to his place. Fucking *now.*"

"*Randy* did? What the hell's going on?"

"I have to tell you something."

Sean explained as we drove: "There was no deal."

"Huh?"

"Randy wasn't expecting us. I never called him." He sighed, a heavy, hopeless sound. "I've been so pissed with him."

"We've all been. But what—?"

"When you found that soda can all I thought about was the money. But talking about Randy so much, lately, has really fucked me up. And I got to thinking about revenge."

"You're losing me."

"Listen—you didn't want to sell the dope. Neither did I. But flushing all the money would be crazy. We could sell it to Randy, but why give him a good opportunity? And he'd rip us off, anyhow. Then I thought about my high school law class. A cop came in, one day, talking about Crime Stoppers— you know, where you report crimes anonymously, and get a cash reward. Up to a thousand bucks.

"So I figured, 'The cops want Randy. They raided the employee lockers at the plant trying to nail him.' Except, he got away. But if we stashed that dope in Randy's house, then called Crime Stoppers, we would be rid of the drugs, Randy would get it in the ass, and we'd be up a thousand bucks."

I felt nauseated. "But he found the shit before the cops got there."

"I think that's what happened."

"And he probably thinks I was in on this, too."

"Yeah."

"Holy fuck."

I pulled in front of Randy's house. Across the street a teenaged boy mowed a lawn; kids played hopscotch a ways up the sidewalk. A man washed his car a few houses away. And I wondered if they had any idea who lived within shouting distance of their families, using them as camouflage.

Before getting out of the car I said, "First thing, you tell Randy I wasn't part of your fucking plan."

"I'll try," Sean said. "But *you* stashed the shit."

"But you—" The words died in my throat, recalling that gun in the drawer.

We went to the house. Sean knocked on the door. "It's open," Randy barked. I followed Sean inside.

Randy sat in the living room, glaring at us. Held the gun in one hand, and some plastic pouches from the soda can in his other hand. "Sit down," he said.

We sat on the couch; I couldn't take my eyes off that gun.

Sean said, "Before you say anything—"

"Shut the fuck up," Randy spat. "I'm going to make this easy to understand."

We stared at him. That fucking gun.

"Nobody fucks with me." He held out the handful of drugs. "Do you know what this is?"

"Cocaine," Sean said.

"Wrong. It's a genie—it'll get me *any*thing I want. I give it to the right person, and you're both dead and dumped in the river by the end of the night."

I closed my eyes.

"I'm not gonna do that—at least not yet. Two reasons. First, this is smack—heroin. There's enough in that soda can to pay off some debts." He leered at us. "In some fucked-up way you did me a favor." The smile disappeared. "Second, you're gonna make a pick-up for me Saturday night."

"Where," Sean asked.

"You got a gig at O'Rourke's, in Detroit, Saturday night. The owner'll give you a package. Bring it to me. When I have it, maybe I'll forget about this."

"What'll he give us?" Sean said.

"Ask another question, you little prick, and I'll blow your fucking head off," Randy said. "You bring me what he gives you."

We said nothing until I'd driven halfway up the block. My mind swung between the poles of my probable fate: jail or death.

"I'm sorry," Sean said. "If I thought there was even a chance . . ." he trailed off.

I turned the corner.

"I'll call Randy—"

"You're a fucking liar!" I shouted. "He threatened our *lives!* What the fuck were you thinking?"

"If you'd stashed the shit like I told you to, he'd be in jail right now!"

I slammed the brakes; heard the screech of tires behind us. Grabbed Sean by the shirt. "You lied!" I shouted. "What were you thinking?" Horns blared behind us.

"We're blocking traffic."

"Fuck that!"

Sean knocked my hand away, and got out of the car. I pulled to the curb. Went after him. The passenger of a passing car shouted, "Asshole!"

I flipped him the finger. "Fuck you!"

I caught up to Sean.

"I was angry," he said. "I was so pissed—I wanted to get him back. That's all. I hated him and I wanted to fuck him up."

"Well, you fucked *us* up. How could you lie to me about this?"

"You wouldn't have gone along."

"You're goddamned right!"

Sean frowned. "Why did you even bring that shit to my place?"

I had no answer.

"We'll do what Randy wants," Sean said.

"He was talking about us bringing drugs over the border," I said. "If we're caught, we're done. Not only jail, Randy'll have someone come after us for losing the drugs to the cops. He knows people."

"Then trust me to fix this."

The three days between our meeting with Randy, and the gig in Detroit, were excruciating. I attended my classes at the university; did all I could to distract myself from thinking about our errand. The rest of the band were excited about playing in Detroit; some even had kind words about Randy being a good guy arranging the gig. I said nothing. Bruce and Danny, the drummer, even registered our instruments with Canada Customs so there would be no hassle at the border.

I couldn't decide if Sean was confident, or suicidal. "We can do this," he said to me on the phone the night before heading to Detroit. "Upwards of thirty thousand cars cross every weekend. I've read that in the paper. Odds are in our favor to get through."

Having no idea what size package we'd be given, it was difficult planning how to smuggle it. One thing was sure: we wouldn't involve the band.

The night of the show Sean and I drove to Detroit in my Dodge Omni, with our guitars in the hatchback. Bruce, and the other guys, went in his ten-year-old station wagon: drum kit, accordion, *bodhrán*, soundboard, flute and tin whistles piled in the back. We crossed the Ambassador Bridge at six in the evening, leaving plenty of time for set up and a sound check. Randy's directions were clear enough, and by half past the hour we got to O'Rourke's. The owner met us at the door.

I had anticipated him being like Randy: an old sneering, hippie wreck. In fact, Kevin O'Rourke was a slight, balding man in his forties, dressed in black slacks, burgundy blazer, shirt and tie. He was quick to smile, and seemed rather amiable, having a couple of doormen help us lug in the equipment. As we set up, Kevin said we'd be paid three hundred dollars and could drink all the free beer we wanted.

"We're playing here again—soon," Bruce said, after Kevin had walked away.

By eighty-thirty we had set up and finished the sound check. Took a table near the stage and ordered a few pitchers of beer. While the guys drank I got up, and looked for Kevin. Found him at the bar.

"The turn-out's looking good," he said. "People can't get enough Irish music!"

I said, "You have a package for us?"

"We'll square-up at the end of the night."

The band finished three pitchers of beer by the time we took the stage at nine-thirty—the waitress made sure we never ran dry—and played better than we had in weeks. The crowd cheered every song. At some point I managed to forget—*ignore* might be a better word—what brought us there, and settled in to enjoying the show. We did our usual three sets, taking two twenty minute breaks, and played right up to last-call at two a.m.

We took our time packing up, and finishing the beer after the show. By quarter to three the bar was empty.

The doormen helped us bring the equipment out to the cars. When everything had been packed away, Kevin came to the door. Handed me three hundred dollars in fifties, which I handed to Bruce—if we got stopped I didn't want the guys to get stiffed for the money.

"Hold on a second," Kevin said, as a waitress came out with six take-out cartons. "Can't let you go away hungry." He directed the waitress to hand the cartons to me. "Thanks for a great night, guys." With that the front door slammed behind us, and there we stood on the sidewalk. I felt like I was holding a bomb.

Danny reached for one of the cartons.

"We'll dig in when we get home," I said.

As the guys headed to Bruce's car, Sean stopped them.

"What're you talking about?" Bruce said when Sean asked him to drive the guys back in my car. "We go back in the cars we came in."

"I need you to do me this favor."

"The four of us in that little car," Bruce said. "That's stupid."

"Do it!" Sean shouted.

Bruce handed over the car keys. "Whatever you say." I gave him my keys, and he and the guys drove off.

"Why's he always got to make me yell?" Sean said. I shook my head. I was tired.

We got into the station wagon—Sean was driving—and opened the take-out cartons. At first glance they appeared to contain a hamburger with a side order of French fries. But digging through the cold fries I uncovered six golf ball-sized plastic bags filled with white powder, fastened with yellow twist ties.

"They're probably all like that," Sean said.

"Doesn't seem like much."

"They wouldn't risk giving us a couple of kilos. He's probably just trying us out on this run. If we don't get pinched at the border, he might demand we cross more shit."

"Do this again." A jolt of anxiety speared through. "But he said he'd forget about everything if we did this for him!"

Sean looked at me. "We're not in a position to argue with him."

"Jesus Christ." I covered the plastic baggies with the French fries. "In the base drum?"

We got out, and stacked the cartons in the bass drum.

"And if Customs checks back here, and smell the food?" I said.

"Nobody'll look in there."

By the time we got to the Ambassador Bridge tollbooths, I sat on my hands to keep them still. He paid the toll and pulled onto the bridge. And panic hit me full force.

"We'll get through, right," I asked.

"Sure." He didn't look at me.

As we cruised across the empty bridge, I thought of Randy's words, *I give it to the right person and you're both dead and dumped in the river by the end of the night . . .*

Looking at Windsor spread out before us, the lights of the border check, of Huron Church Road just beyond.

"Jesus Christ," Sean said, slowing the car.

"What's the matter?"

"There were hardly any cars at the toll booths," he said. "And there probably won't be many at Customs."

"You think we'll be pulled over?"

He looked at me.

"Oh God," I said. "We're dead!"

"Listen," Sean said. "I'm gonna stop. You go around back, fasten the cartons inside the drum—Bruce might have a roll of friction tape under all that shit. Then throw the drum over the railing. And do it *fast!*"

"Somebody will see!"

"We gotta try."

He stopped when we were above the shoreline, and handed me the keys. "Go!"

I ran around the car and opened the back, searching for something to secure the cartons. There was nothing. We were going to be caught—

—I had a thought.

Took off my jacket, pulled off my denim shirt, spreading it on top of the drum. And emptied the cartons into it. I tied the sleeves, collar, and bottom of the shirt together, making a bundle. Raced to the bridge's railing and flung it over. Then tossed over the cartons.

Turning to the car, I saw Sean had raised the hood and was looking over the engine. For a second I actually thought the car had conked-out, but when I got in the car and slammed the door, he shut the hood and jumped in, too. I gave him the keys.

Seeing my undershirt under my jacket, he said, "You used your *shirt?*"

"Had to use something."

"What? Why didn't you fasten it inside the drum and heave *it* over?"

"The drum would've exploded hitting the water. Everything would've sunk."

"But your shirt's too light! The wind'll take it. Christ, it probably got blown right into the river."

"There's hardly any wind."

"Doesn't take much to carry a shirt."

"It could be carried toward shore, too," I said, as we approached the inspection booths of Canada Customs.

Two booths were open. Five cars waited ahead of us. None of them took very long with the Customs officer, and I felt a spark of hope that we'd be simply waved through. It was not long before the car ahead pulled out. Sean rolled up to the booth.

The Customs officer was a woman in her thirties. We showed our identification.

"How long away," she asked.

"A few hours," Sean said.

"Where are you coming from?"

"We stayed for last-call at O'Rourke's."

My stomach felt like a deflating balloon.

"It's an Irish bar in downtown Detroit," Sean added.

The Customs officer looked us over. "Go ahead."

Sean pulled through, and turned right onto Huron Church Road. We headed toward the waterfront.

I felt weightless, detached. Released my breath. "We got through."

"Now for some real fun," Sean said. "Finding those fucking baggies."

To the left of the Ambassador Bridge, at the waterfront, was a nursing home called Villa Marie. Sean pulled into its parking lot, which extended nearly to the river.

"We're no further ahead if the shirt's lost in the water," Sean said.

We got out of the car. Sean headed to the shore, while I searched the dark, sloping lawn. I wished we had brought a flashlight.

Maybe it was the hour of the night, or my fatigue, or panic, but I got thinking about the winter I was eight years old. Remembered my mother sending a friend and me to the corner store one evening. When we got back to house, my mother's change was gone. Couldn't figure what had happened to it. Searched all my pockets—nothing. Told my mother it must have fallen out when I pulled my gloves from my pockets. Then offered to give it to her two dollars from my piggy bank.

"No," she had said. "I want *my* two dollars." With that, my friend and I were sent back outside to find the missing money.

It had been dark and windy that evening. There was no way we'd find the money if it had, actually, fallen out of my pocket; wondering what my mother would say when we returned without the two dollars. As my friend and I approached the end of my street, I found a dollar bill lying in the snow by a tree. Further up the sidewalk we found another. Must've fallen out when I pulled my gloves from my pocket, just like I thought. I couldn't believe my luck. Neither had my mother.

And I wondered what we would tell Randy if we didn't find the baggies. Would he believe they were lost? Would he even care what we said? I felt sick.

Lost in my reverie, I nearly walked into the bare branches of a small blossom tree. Looked up, startled. Did a double-take, unable to believe what I saw: my shirt hanging among the branches like a broken kite.

"Found it," I called, stunned, elated.

I searched the ground underneath the tree and found a bag of dope.

"Jesus Christ, they're all over the place," Sean said, as he came alongside me.

"We only looked in the two cartons," I said, picking up another bag from the grass. "Do you figure there were six baggies in each of them?"

"Fuck if I know."

I found another baggie, caught on a low-hanging branch. It was torn and most of the contents had spilled out.

"Great," Sean said.

"What's he gonna say if we're short?"

"Fuck him," Sean said, walking around the other side of the tree. He bent down and picked something up. It was a piece of broken Styrofoam cup.

Of the thirty-six baggies we assumed were hidden in the take-out cartons, we found twenty-two. And three of those were either punctured, or ripped open. I climbed into the tree and got my denim shirt—and wrapped the baggies we'd found in it. Then we went back to the car.

I could not figure why we stopped at Sean's house, before heading to Randy's. Sean jumped out, leaving the car running, and headed into the garage: a slanted wooden structure behind the house. He reappeared carrying a paper bag.

"What's that?" I asked, as we pulled out of the driveway.

"Something to even our odds."

We drove in silence and parked a block from Randy's house—Sean didn't want him to know we were coming. I grabbed the baggies bundled in my shirt. Sean stopped me.

"Only bring one," he said.

"Why?"

"Leave the rest here until we find out if we're still on his shit-list." Sean reached into the paper bag, and pulled out a gun.

"What the fuck?" I breathed.

"My dad worked for an armored car company and had to

provide his own gun. Kept it after he quit. I went home the day before last and got it from his lockbox in the closet. He won't miss it."

"But Randy won't give us trouble," I said. "Not after we did this for him."

"I'm not taking any more chances with that cocksucker."

There were no lights at Randy's house. It stood dark and quiet as any other on the block. We knocked on the door, rang the doorbell and waited. And waited. No answer.

"Bastard's probably sleeping," Sean muttered. He pounded loudly on the door.

We waited. And waited. No answer.

"He can't expect us to hold onto this shit," I said.

"Might have to let ourselves in," Sean said, heading around the back of the house. "Leave him the bag, and a note."

The rear door was locked—the pane near the doorknob was broken. Sean reached through and opened the door.

"This isn't good," he whispered, and went inside. I followed.

The basement door lay directly ahead. The light was on down there. Sean slowly descended the staircase. And he was the first to see it, gasping, hand against the wall, turning his head, and vomiting. It was the odor that hit me first: the scorched stink of burnt hair. I looked passed Sean and felt my legs nearly go out from beneath me.

Randy sat slumped over his desk, the front of his skull blown away: blood and brains and skull splattered nakedly across the recording equipment. Shot in the back of the head: what the cops on TV called *execution style.*

We fled the house, cutting through the backyard to the alley, running down to the side street where we left the station wagon. I tossed the bag of dope with the others at my feet. Sean shoved the gun under his seat. As we pulled away from the curb, I saw that he was crying.

When you've actually lived through it, stories like this have no ending. There's no end-music, no closing credits. The story continues in the mind even when you stop running, when enemies disappear, been murdered. And that early morning when I picked up the soda can, haunts me with the same vivid intensity as the sight of Randy Kurzuk slumped over his desk, dead.

Sean and I drove from Randy's house to the waterfront. We went to the end of the concrete pier beneath the Ambassador Bridge, and tossed the dope into the river.

Randy's murderer was never found, so the newspaper has said up to now. I have no guesses. He was a bad guy.

The band's master tape sits in my dresser drawer. I don't know if they still argue over money: where to get it, how to spend it—I haven't played with them in two months; since all this happened. I don't know if I'm angry with Sean. I just don't want to see him again. I had called Danny days after our gig at O'Rourke's, and told him I was done with it: the bickering, concerns over cash, where to play, on and on. He seemed to understand.

In the days following Randy's murder the cops contacted us, asked about our dealings with him. It didn't take them long to figure we had nothing to offer other than complaints about Randy's incompetence as a recording technician. Bruce called me a few days afterward, asking if I knew anything about our master tape. I guess he asked the cops if we could have it back. They gave him the telephone number of the lawyer inventorying Randy's belongings; the lawyer said he never came across it. Maybe I should have told Bruce that I have it, but for some reason I didn't.

I think about calling Sean once in a while, wondering if he's kept up nights, too, recalling Randy slumped over his desk, blood and brains exploded all over the place. To see if he wonders what might have happened to us if we hadn't stopped on the bridge; if we had gone straight to Randy's house from the bridge. Wondering if Randy might still be alive, or if we would have died with him.

Last Saturday night I went to O'Rourke's Pub. An Irish band was playing—our band was better. Didn't see Kevin, anywhere. Hanging-out by the bar, I watched people all night leaving with take-out cartons. I left around midnight.

There were few cars on the Ambassador Bridge coming home. After crossing the midway point, I slowed and stopped roughly where Sean and I had stopped two months ago. Switched on my hazard lights, got out, and went to the railing. Looking down on the quiet, well-lit streets of west Windsor, the breeze blowing on my face, it all seemed so peaceful and orderly.

As My Sparks Fly Upward

It has all come together. Doesn't seem possible: a year of waiting and my Irish passport came through last month. In less than a week I'll be on a trans-Atlantic flight to Dublin, where I plan to live and write and work.

"What are your prospects in Ireland?" a friend of my parents' asked me a few weeks ago.

"I'll see when I arrive," I had said, rather than expounding upon the toxic familiarity of Windsor. Having spent a few summers traveling Ireland, I figured it was as good a place as any to flee following graduation.

This is my last Saturday night in town.

Driving down University Street to meet friends at the University of Windsor's campus pub—once a large private residence, but has since been turned into the Grad House—my mind lights with memory. Passing Curry Avenue I think of Jessica Fountain, the girl I loved through elementary school. Sandy blonde hair, green eyes, freckles, hint of a lisp softening her "S's." Hardly said a word to her in those early days. Although we became something close to friends in high school, nothing ever came of it. We walked home from high school together once in a while, talked on the telephone.

I'll never forget nights riding my bike past her house, seeing the lights in the windows, wondering which was hers. Some nights her older sister was on the porch with friends and I'd just pedal by. One evening in the autumn of sixth grade I biked past and saw Jessica sitting alone on her porch. I was about to go by when she called my name. I slowed, coasted up the walk. Can't recall what we talked about, but sitting there on my bike, looking at Jessica in the fading dusk, I decided that anything that felt so natural and good had to be love.

It's a clear night tonight, cool for early May—every year winter seems to sprawl further into spring. Still I drive with the window open. Never realized how much I missed the air having fragrance after the frozen banality of winter.

Josephine Avenue. Years reel backward to the days of prowling the neighborhood with my best friend, Jamie Gillard. We were ten. First started listening to the radio with Jamie in the basement bedroom he shared with his older brother, Dave. Back then we could barely distinguish The Who from The Rolling Stones, Jimi Hendrix from Eric Clapton. Always wondering what our favorite bands looked like; finding pictures of Jim Morrison, Led Zeppelin, Neil Young in rock magazines was like stumbling upon the Shroud of Turin. In fifth grade I had a T-shirt with a blurred concert photo of Led Zeppelin on the front and remember kids at school asking me which member of the band was "Led."

Heard my first concert in Jamie's basement: Sammy Hagar at Cobo Hall, broadcast live on the radio.

First saw a naked woman there, too, looking through his brother's *Penthouse* and *Hustler* magazines. Smoked my first cigarette with Jamie in the alley behind our elementary school. And sleeping over at his house, staying up all night talking about girls we liked, guys we wanted to fight, he was the only person I ever told about Jessica. He laughed, but was okay. He kept the secret.

And the years have a way of robbing people. Jamie was held back to repeat fifth grade. By high school he was another face I nodded to in the hallway. Should look him up before I leave. Always meant to give him a call.

*   *   *

University Street is quiet tonight. All the action's downtown, and just as well.

Turning onto Sunset Avenue, where the darkened buildings of the university stand, it's hard to believe I trod through six years here: forty-five courses, innumerable afternoons and nights lost at the Grad House; the poetry readings, faculty parties. Completed my Master's Degree last November. Been working since, earning my airfare to Ireland. Seems like a long time since I was last on campus. February was it? March? Feels like forever since I last saw my friends.

The Grad House isn't busy tonight; on weekends everybody goes to the dance clubs downtown. I park out front and head inside. After a quick look around the bar, I see my friends haven't yet arrived. Order a pitcher of Rickard's Red and head out to the patio. Fill my glass and look at the quiet neighborhood.

And think about one autumn evening I spent here two years ago, following my first day as graduate assistant. Came here directly from the expository writing class I taught, stomach still sick with nerves, mind full of the twenty staring faces of the students. Had a late lunch, some drinks with friends who stopped by between classes. I had the rest of the day off and spent it here on the patio, into the evening and night.

When full dark came, I got to looking at the stars and thinking they weren't stars at all but sparks of memory, experiences lodged in the firmament. That, in the night sky above the park where I first kissed a girl, one of those glowing pinpricks held that moment. Above the neighborhood where I lived as a kid, above Jessica Fountain's house where I first fell in love, above Dillon Hall where I taught my first writing class—one of those brilliant specks in the sky held each particular moment.

And I must have been drunker than I thought about then

because a line from the Bible came to mind; the only one I knew by memory. Half a line, really: ". . . as sparks fly upward . . ." And was possessed by a sense, a depression of sorts, that had trailed me through high school, through most of my undergraduate years: the distance between my present-self and child-self was widening every day, and all the old friends and good times were not only gone, but fading forever. That old lost-feeling took hold whenever I saw Jamie in the high school hallways, or saw Jessica walking through the cafeteria. It fell upon me again that autumn night.

And it's here, now, though I seek consolation thinking about the permanence of the stars—

"He's drunk already."

Mike and Jen and Chris approach the table.

"This your second or third pitcher?" Mike says.

"Just got here," I say, filling glasses.

Talk of the English department fills the first while. Details of the spring graduate defenses: Chris just completed his, Mike and Jen are set to go next week. Halfway through the first round of drinks conversation turns to the future: doctoral programs in distant cities, crossed fingers and letters of recommendation, transcripts and grant applications. Soon the first pitcher is gone and money is dropped into the jukebox.

"Any new entries for the Tales of Modern Horror?" Chris asks me.

I don't know precisely when it began, but I have become known as a collector of morbid true-life stories. Chris has suggested on more than one occasion that I collect them in an anthology titled, *Tales of Modern Horror.*

"This isn't really a Tale of Modern Horror," I say, refilling my glass, "but I was just thinking. On my way here I passed my old grade school and remembered breaking into the place with my little brother and a friend named Timmy Murphy.

"It was a Sunday in May and we were bored. We went to the schoolyard, throwing rocks at a mesh box covering the recess bell, when I noticed the window of the boys' bathroom, on the second floor was half-open. I got this idea about walking along the ledge to that window, climbing in and letting the other two into the school—one of those stupid ideas that seems so logical when you're nine.

"I talked Timmy Murphy into climbing a fence onto the first floor roof of the kindergarten classroom. He crossed that roof to the wall of the second floor and walked along the ledge—it couldn't have been more than a foot wide, at least fifteen feet in the air, and about twenty yards to the half-open window. Christ, he would have been paralyzed if he'd fallen.

"But he didn't fall, and there he was, performing the most conspicuous break-in in the history of crime. He got into the school and let us in. Once inside the school, the guys looked at me as if to say, 'What now?' I had no idea. So we ran, full-tilt, through the hallways, screaming our heads off.

"My younger brother went about five steps from the door, then turned back. Tim and I ran through the halls, into the gym and finally out a side door. We headed back to my house, figuring my brother would be there.

"Except he wasn't. Just then my parents came out of the house, taking the dog for a walk. Not long after a neighborhood kid came by. He said, 'They know you did it. You can either go back to the school, or they'll come here.' Jesus! Then he turned and left.

"We went back. Like walking to the gallows. I guess somebody living near the school saw Tim crawl into the window, called the cops, then ran over to catch us. When my brother ran out, he was nabbed. Except my brother didn't tell the cops right off who the other kids were. When my parents went by with the dog, they saw him talking with the cops, figured he was a witness to a break-in, but not involved. Then Tim and I showed up.

"The cops took our names and sent us home with my parents. I was grounded for a month. My brother got off light because he ran out of the school. Tim was taken home in a police car.

"The next day at school everybody knew about it. Tim's older brother spread the story around the night before. Tim and I were in the same class. First thing that morning, our teacher took us in the hallway, asking what in God's name had possessed us to break into the school. Our classmates looked at us like we had killed somebody. In the schoolyard the older kids looked at us with a mixture of amazement and something like admiration. No one in recent memory had done something that *awful* since one of the Lockwood kids told a teacher to fuck off a few years before.

"After recess we were called down to The Office on the P.A.—like being summoned to Heinrich Himmler's office. Seemed as though the whole school held its breath. This was it. Time for Punishment.

"We passed an older kid in the hall. He grinned at us and said, 'Sister's gonna kill you!'

"We got to The Office and Sister Gladys Moran—*Moron*, the kids called her; a real peach—gave us a rambling lecture about shaming our families, staining our good names. It sounded like a mixture of Deuteronomy and *Mein Kampf.* Then she brought out The Strap—equivalent to a firing squad, as far as I was concerned. No kid ever got strapped and *not* cried. Not even the Lockwood kid."

"There was a whole folklore surrounding The Strap at my school," Chris says. "Stories of the principal accidentally smashing a kid in the side of the face with it, tearing out an eye."

"We had the same thing," Jen says. "Like if you put hairs across your palms, your hands would split wide open on the first lash. Then you could sue the school."

"Same here," I say. "When Sister got The Strap I put a few hairs across my left palm, figuring I'd quit school on the money I would get from the multi-million dollar lawsuit. Well, my hand didn't split open. After being Strapped, we dutifully cried. Then went back class. And heading down the hallway I felt different. Giddy, in a strange, stupid way. I had survived. Became part of The Strap's folklore. Lost my virginity, in a way."

"Was it all dropped after that?" Jen asks.

"Pretty much. Except, two weeks later one of the older kids said to me. 'So, you really broke into the school?' I said yeah. He grinned, 'I should tell.' I was amazed. *Every*body knew. When I told him that, he looked disappointed he wouldn't get the chance to blackmail me."

By one a.m. we've finished our fourth pitcher of beer, and are ready to head out for some food.

"Where to now?" Chris asks. We walk to my car and pile in.

"How about Diana's?" Mike says.

A gyro and fries would go down like a dream about now.

Diana's Pizzeria sits on the corner of University and Josephine. The place is half-full. We take a table near the windows. The waitress comes by with menus, says she'll be back in a second with some water. And the exhilaration I felt leaving the Grad House mingles with a rising urgency: I'm leaving everything, everyone around me, in a few days. Suddenly it's important that I tell Mike and Jen and Chris more about Jamie Gillard, more about Jessica Fountain, more about everything, so that nothing is forgotten.

"You believe my story about breaking into the school, don't you?" I say.

"Sure," Mike says, perusing a menu. Jen nods.

"Why?" Chris says.

"It's just . . . it's important that you believe it." My appetite wavers and disappears. I don't want to eat, I want to talk, remember, resurrect.

"Relax," Jen says, patting my shoulder.

I smile, feeling jittery and anxious. And as I am about to mention that Josephine Avenue is where Jamie Gillard livee, my eyes fall on a face across the room as familiar to me as my own.

"Holy Jesus," I say.

It's Jessica Fountain.

I approach the table where she sits with three other girls. Her hair is longer than when I last saw her; she looks great.

She looks up, startled. Doesn't recognize me at first. Then her expression melts into a smile. "Hey, how're you doing?"

"Great," I say, then blurt out: "I'm moving to Ireland next week."

"Ireland?" she says. She actually sounds surprised, interested, and I'm suddenly wondering why I haven't given her a call. "That's great—"

"Listen, you've got to meet my friends!"

"Well, I've—"

"It'll only take a second. Come on."

"Maybe some other time."

"I'd really like you to."

She thinks about it. Her friends don't seem particularly moved by my request. Jessica looks at me and the smile fades a little from her eyes. "Good luck in Ireland," she says.

"Okay. Good seeing you."

Back to the table; sheepish, stinging, explaining I was just talking to Jessica Fountain, marveling at seeing her, here, tonight. The waitress passes our table, approaches Jessica and her friends, shuffling through a stack of bills; places a bill on their table. And a certain irony dawns on me: the uncountable nights during my visit to Ireland last year where strangers became friends in the course of a night, over a few rounds of drinks, and here I am, seeing old friends and am unable to spark any sort of conversation; there being no glimmer of reminiscence between us.

"What's the matter?" Jen asks.

I turn. She's looking at me; so are Chris and Mike. "You all right?" Chris asks.

"I guess. It's just . . . the night can't end like this, not here." That old lost-feeling creeps in.

"Where do you want to go?" Mike says.

"I don't know." I turn and watch Jessica and her friends rise from the table. Jessica waves as she leaves. I wave her over. She says something to her friends, who nod and continue out.

"Thanks," I say as she approaches. "I just wanted my friends to meet you—we were telling stories about grade school and I couldn't believe seeing you here."

I introduce her around the table; everyone nods and says hello.

"Jamie's here," she says.

"Jamie Gillard?" I look around for him.

"He went into the bathroom a minute ago. You must've walked right past him," Jessica says. "I talked to him when he came in. He's back from orthodontic college, visiting his family. There he is." Jessica points over my shoulder. I turn and see Jamie emerge from the restrooms.

Mustache, thinning hair. Huskier than when I last saw him, but looking well.

"Well, for Christ's sake," I mutter, getting up, maneuvering around a few tables and grabbing him by the shoulder. He looks at me with the same startled expression Jessica had. I throw my arms around him in a bear hug.

"Jesus, Jamie," I say. "It's good to see you."

"What the fuck—?" He pushes me away, startled, frowning. Then he recognizes me, grabs me in a bear hug. "Man, where'd you come from? It's good to see *you.*"

I bring him to the table and introduce him around. As the greetings end Jessica puts a hand on my arm and says, "I've got to go."

"Thanks for coming over," I say, wondering if I should shake her hand or embrace her. I do neither.

"Good luck."

Jamie says, "Listen, you gotta meet my wife. Why don't we get one table for all of us?"

"You're married?"

"Two years now."

My mind reels. "I've got to meet Mrs. Gillard."

Mike and Chris push a couple of tables together. Jamie's wife is a petite woman with a strong Italian nose, dark eyes and hair, and an entrancing smile. Her name is Daphna. She studies filmmaking in Toronto.

"If we run into Tim Murphy," Mike says, "I'll eat this chair."

The waitress comes around and takes our orders. And my appetite finds its way back by the time the food comes. We eat and talk, and when Jamie finishes his cheeseburger, he rises from the table. "Is everybody heading home from here?" he asks. "Or do you feel like doing something after this?"

Glance at my watch: it's a few minutes past two.

"What do have you in mind?" Chris says.

"Tell you when I get back." Jamie looks at Daphna. "Be

back in a minute."

Through the window I watch him cross University Street and jog up Josephine Avenue. He returns a few minutes later with two paper bags.

"Party aid," he announces, panting from his run. He pulls a three-quarter-full, forty-ounce bottle of vodka from the bags.

"Where did you get that?" Mike says.

"My folks live around the corner."

"We can't drink in here," I say.

"So let's pay the bill and go where we can," Jamie says.

Reaching for my car keys outside, I see someone coming down the sidewalk, about thirty yards away: a young night-club-goer probably abandoned by her friends downtown. Everyone piles into the car; Mike is relegated to the hatch back. As I slide into the driver's seat someone calls my name.

It's the person approaching.

She steps into the light of Diana's windows. It's Jessica.

"What brought you back?" I say, going to her.

"I thought about how glad you were seeing me. It's been so long . . . and you're leaving soon."

"Hop in."

"Where are you going?"

"Haven't figured that out yet, but you're coming too."

"The car's already full."

"Plenty of room."

It's decided she'll sit on Jen's lap.

"Where are we going to drink?" Chris says.

"The river front?" Jamie says.

"We'll have to watch for cops making their rounds," Jen says. "Every high school kid in town goes there with a stash of beer."

A thought comes to mind. I smile. *Of course.*

"I know a place," I say, putting the car in gear and pulling a U-turn in the empty street.

"It better not be far," Mike croaks from the hatchback. "The gyro I ate isn't taking kindly to the fetal position."

I make a quick detour to an all-night convenience store to buy a stack of plastic cups, a bottle of Coke, bottle of orange juice and a bag of ice.

"Mike," I say, opening the hatchback, "we're counting on you to sacrifice some of your space for the supplies."

"Martyrs get first crack at the booze!"

Cameron Avenue. Every house is dark and still. Halfway up the block is the darkened building of Sacred Heart elementary school. I swing into the empty parking lot, through the open gates into the schoolyard, and park by the rear doors Tim Murphy opened for my brother and I sixteen years ago. The two-story main building of the school is at our right; the one-floor wing—giving the school its L-shape—is at our left. Privacy.

"We have arrived," I say, shutting off the engine, but turning the ignition back to run the battery. Switch on the radio to a Detroit rock 'n' roll station, and leave the hatch open, where I assemble the bag of ice and booze and mix in a row: an impromptu bar. Pass around the plastic cups. Mike mixes himself a rye and Coke; the girls go for vodka and orange juice. I pour myself a rye and ice. Sipping drink.

"So, this is the scene of the great caper," Chris says. He's drinking vodka and Coke.

I look at the two-story main building, point at the narrow ledge running the school's length fifteen feet above. "Tim walked along that ledge to those windows."

Chris shakes his head, smiling. "I'm glad I didn't know

120

you in grade school."

"Tim could've broken his neck."

I turn to Jessica. "There's our first-grade classroom," I say, nodding at the darkened windows behind us.

"Seemed to take forever for the term to end," Mike says. "Now I can only remember bits and pieces of grade school."

"I never thought we'd make it out of here alive," Jamie says. We laugh. I remember.

The talk continues and the drinks go down. With sudden, fleeting clarity I realize I'm drunk. This pleases me, for some reason. I pour another drink and note that there will be enough booze for a few more.

Jamie tells Mike and Jen and Chris about us getting into trouble throwing snowballs, tripping girls, taking a kid's new football and playing keep-away. As he talks, remembering stories, I look to Jessica. I'm reminded of the Friday night dances in seventh and eighth grade, how I wished I had the guts to ask her for a dance—and never did. Recalling the dim gymnasium decorated with paper streamers, colored lights flashing from the stage; a strobe light switched on during the fast songs. Primitive and gaudy compared to the dance clubs downtown, but something happened on those nights that has never been captured in any nightclub I ever saw; a feeling in the air, circulating through everybody in the gym.

Jessica looks at me. Smiles. I lean close. "I thought about you all the time in grade school."

"Yeah?" Something in her smile says she always knew.

"Always hoped we'd be together by high school," I say, "but I didn't know how to make it happen."

"You should've just asked," she says.

I hear Jamie telling the others about the time we were kept in after school and climbed out of the window of the first-floor classroom when the teacher left the room. Nearly got suspended for that one.

And I am possessed by a sense, something I once felt . . . haven't felt since being here, since those dances in seventh and eighth grade; that excitement, exhilaration that would leap out of the air and seize me by the throat. I feel it now. Looking at the school, it seems more like a tomb. Not exactly a tomb, but a place of waiting; a place for ghosts. Waiting for the doors to be flung open and someone to shout, "I remember! I remember it all!"

Ghosts. Of course. They've been tugging at me all night. Jessica Fountain. Jamie Gillard. And here they are with me—finally.

But the ghosts? They're still trapped inside the school. I can almost see Jessica and Jamie and me—our nine year-old selves—and our classmates gathered beyond the windows, staring, hands outstretched toward the moonlight, toward the stars: those glowing pinpricks of experience, memory. I begin to realize what this feeling of exhilaration is pushing me toward.

I toss my empty cup into the hatchback and jog toward the chain-link fence hedging-in the teachers' parking lot. It's fastened at a post by the corner of the single-floor building.

Chris calls to me, "What're you doing?"

I climb the seven-foot fence. Steadying myself with a hand on the wall of the school, I stand on the top crossbar. The roof is about two and-a-half feet above my head. I grab hold, feeling the cool aluminum trim bordering the roof, the rubbery texture of the tar sealant and pebbles scattered along the roof; I always wondered why the pebbles were there.

Pulling myself up, getting my upper torso over the edge, I swing my leg up, catch the aluminum edge with my shoe and roll onto the roof. I lay here for a moment, looking into the clear sky; looking at the stars containing every schoolyard fight, every great catch made in a touch-football game, every furtive scaling of this roof.

"What are you doing?" Mike calls.

Cross the roof toward the two-story main building, and approach the ledge. It's so narrow; can't be any more than fourteen or fifteen inches wide.

Jen calls my name; sounds worried. "What're you doing?"

"Come and have another drink," Jamie shouts. "One slip and you'll be going to Ireland in a body cast."

Step onto the ledge—facing the wall, shuffling sideways—balancing myself by holding onto the narrow steel beams framing the classroom windows.

There is the sound of footsteps moving along the pebbled roof. Look over my shoulder and see Mike has climbed up. Calls my name. I continue along the ledge, away from the roof.

"Go down by the doors!" I shout over my shoulder. "I'll be there in a minute."

Shuffling along the ledge, I look into the darkness of my fourth grade classroom: thirty empty desks—Jessica sat second from the front in the third row; I sat near the back of the fifth row and had an unobstructed view of her when my classmates were bent over their grammar lessons and math problems. Teacher's desk looms at the front. Fish drowse in an aquarium by the windows.

Come upon the sixth grade classroom: plants lining the rear counter; bulletin board opposite the windows full of art-work. Nothing notable happened in sixth grade, except for one thing: I sat behind Jessica that entire year. Sometimes the deities in charge of bad luck nod off and let that kind of thing happen. Nearly all meaningful contact I had with her during the years happened in this classroom: asking her for help spelling words I already knew how to spell; asking for help with math problems I already knew how to solve; asking for an extra pen when I had three in my book bag; whispering jokes to her during reading period. By the end of the year I thought there was finally a chance she would be my girlfriend; but poor seating arrangements in seventh and eighth grade put the *kibosh* on that. The deities in charge of bad luck don't sleep forever.

My friends call my name.

"Don't worry!" I shout.

Having come about twenty yards along the ledge I am prepared to break the window if it's locked. A nasty, needlessly destructive deed, but I have to get to the ghosts. Before drawing back my fist, I check if it's open: I have seen too many sitcoms where the hero nearly kills himself breaking down a door that wasn't locked to begin with. The window is, indeed, slightly ajar. Why not? It would be nearly impossible to notice from the ground and who would go to the trouble of coming up here to check?

More likely, one of the ghosts flipped the latch for me.

I pull the window open and slip inside, instantly assaulted by a heavy ammonia odor. Head out to the hallway. An *EXIT* sign glows above the doors across from the bathroom; another glows at the far end of the hallway, to my left. As I walk toward that far *EXIT* sign I can almost hear the rustling of papers, notebooks being shoved into book bags; or maybe that's fluttering wings, billowing gowns. The ghosts. Gathering.

Wandering down the hallway, I take the staircase to the ground floor. At the foot of the stairs I push open the double doors and turn right—toward the rear doors where everyone waits.

"You fucking idiot!" Jamie says, laughing, as I open the doors. "We came here to drink, not get arrested."

"You probably set off an alarm the minute you stepped in," Jen says.

I turn and run down the unlit hallway, past the staircase, toward the principal's office. The night—occurring in a stream of flashes, realizations—melds into a blur:

Mike calls my name.

"Come on!" I shout, rounding the corner at the principal's office.

Chris lets out a cowboy cry and shouts, "This is a tale of modern horror!"

Footsteps running behind me: the ghosts. Down the hallway to a set of double doors. Beyond is the Resource Center, on the right, the gymnasium on the left.

Laughter, shouting, swearing, the jiggling of door handles—I hear it all behind me. I turn. My friends follow, drinks in hand. Jamie carries the bottle of whisky. Jen grips the bottle of vodka. Chris stands behind them, at the principal's office, playing with the door handle.

"Wait!" someone shouts as I turn to run. "Where are you going?"

"The gym."

Jump-kick the double doors at full stride. The others arrive moment later, spilling drinks, laughing. Chris is gone.

We head into the darkened gym, with its familiar odor of rubber balls and dirty socks, hanging in the air alongside the stale smell of floor cleaner. There is a crackling sound as the P.A. system is switched on. Chris' voice comes over the speakers: "This is Glenn the Ghoul with more Tales of Modern Horror . . ."

He recites stories we have been telling each other for more than a year.

". . . guy goes to his girlfriend's house to meet her family. Goes upstairs to use the bathroom and takes an enormous dump . . . toilet won't flush. Can't leave it there . . . scoops it into a large wad of toilet paper . . . throws it out the window and it lands on the glass roof of the patio where his girlfriend's family is sitting . . ."

We keep the lights off. I take Jessica by the hand and run toward the stage. Feel my way through the door and switch on the stage lights—just as it was during the dances in seventh and eighth grade. Because this is the center. The gymnasium. Place of that old lost-feeling.

I lead Jessica onto the bare stage, and memory flashes brightly, fiercely: Thanksgiving and Christmas pageants in the early grades: playing a pumpkin, an elf; Jessica a pilgrim's wife, a reindeer. Remembrance Day memorials; slideshows of Flanders Fields. School plays. The dances: approaching the DJ with song requests. No matter what songs played, one thought pounded in my mind: Jessica. The sound of her name, the sight of her, the thought, the dream of her. Jessica. The longing tearing at me all through the night: *Go ask her to dance.* But I froze every time.

Jessica. At my side. Now. Smile playing at the corners of her mouth. Breathing deeply after running. Green eyes. Hint of a lisp softening her "S's." Jessica.

Jamie approaches the stage. "We're leaving. You coming?"

"No."

"Maybe we should," Jessica says.

"Not yet," I say.

"Gimme your keys," Jamie says. "I'll put your car on the street."

I toss him the keys; watch everyone leave: Mike and Jen, hear the P.A. switched off. Turn to Jessica, hold her and feel myself sway to songs played here twelve and thirteen years ago. She dances with me, humming something I can't quite make out.

My mind reels, back to the longing that tore through me at every dance. The defeat. Watching her dance with the other guys. Wishing I could—

We kiss. Her eyes close. Her hand cups my neck. My hand slides down to her butt. We kiss. Eyes closed. The soft press of her tongue. We turn and kiss and sway. A soft moan escapes her throat. My other hand moves up from her hips and finds her beast. Her breathing quickens. The moment hangs like the high piercing sound of silence in the empty hallways.

Then a pause. She kisses my neck, runs her tongue under my earlobe. I grip her butt with both hands. The years, nearly two decades, I have dreamed of kissing Jessica.

Opening my eyes, I notice the stack of crash mats piled against the wall at the other side of the stage. Drag it to the center of the stage. And like a couple of kids at a sleepover, we flop onto it. In a flurry of movement we pull off our clothes: the sound of fluttering wings, billowing gowns.

I roll onto Jessica. Naked. With little coaxing I am inside her. She turns her head to the side. A moan escapes her throat. The feeling of wholeness, of victory, of relief soars through me. The blur that this night has is so intensely muddled, the moment is reduced to an inventory from my senses:

Flesh reports intense pleasure; specifics unavailable;

Ears report moans emanating from Jessica, increasing in frequency and volume;

Eyes report Jessica's face turning toward mine, her eyes half-open; hint of a smile curling the corners of her mouth.

She runs her fingernails through my hair. She moves along with my every thrust.

Jessica moans.

Approaching climax. The joining is nearly complete. The part of me that the old lost-feeling once mourned is rising now, lifted onto the shoulders of the ghosts, who point me skyward, star-ward.

Ears report a scream; specifically, Jessica's voice, indicating climax.

Flesh simultaneously reports (painful) raking of fingernails down my back, counterbalancing intensely satisfying coitus release.

Near malfunction of all the senses as my grasp on consciousness becomes tenuous.

It's gotten cold outside. Jessica is at my side.

"Thank God for all the drunks and fights downtown," she says. "Every cop in town must be there."

We head down Martindale Street, which runs perpendicular to Cameron. I am shivering. Jessica stops to help me put on my shirt. My jacket is draped over her shoulders.

"Aren't your legs cold?" she asks and I realize I am not wearing my pants, only my boxer shorts. "I'll help you."

I shake my head. The brief bit of clarity and wakefulness brought on by the cool air is wearing off. Each step requires such effort. I'm stumbling. Feel myself fading.

"It's not much further," Jessica says.

Finally, her house.

"Can we," I say, "sit . . . on your porch . . . for . . . old time's sake?"

Jessica leads me up the walk, we sit on the stairs.

"Goooood," I moan, smiling.

"I am so drunk," she says, giggling. "Me and Jen drank nearly all the vodka."

I lean against her. She puts an arm around me. I think about the stars, wanting to tell her about them. Close my eyes for the last time; there will be no telling. Not tonight.

Cold. My neck and back ache. Must have rolled out of

bed and onto the floor. But it's so cold. Did I leave the window open?

Open my eyes and find that I am not in my bedroom, but on someone's front lawn. A house stands behind me; trees stand above, branches heavy with buds; stars stare down, watchful.

Look to my left and see Jessica curled underneath my jacket. Press the LIGHT button on my wristwatch: it's a few minutes past five a.m.

Mike and Jen and Chris . . . Jamie and Daphna. Where did they go? I'll be making telephone calls in a few hours tracking everyone down, finding out what exactly happened last night. Or is it still tonight?

Jessica stirs. She rolls over, mumbling. I'll let her sleep another minute or two, and then help her into the house. There's still so much to do before leaving. Fresh air must have done me some good because I'm feeling semi-sober. French fries and gyro must have eradicated the hangover—yet again.

The stars are beginning to fade. Thinking about those pinpricks of memory, of Mike and Jen and Chris, about Jamie and Daphna, about Jessica, I know that this evening will live among all the other good nights. Where they'll be safe. Wondering if, when people die, maybe our spirits do journey upward. Maybe we all rise to gather our happy memories among the stars and go off someplace peaceful to enjoy them.

Where Does This Evening Find You?

Back to my breadbox hovel in Drumcondra after an afternoon at the Irish Writers' Centre. Back to the smoke-yellowed walls, carpeting of no distinguishable color, single bed in the corner; broken mirror hanging on the wall—from which the bad luck has surely run out long ago. Back to the tortured blare of Lorkan's TV in the next room, screeching and crackling, seething through the painted-shut double doors separating our rooms.

It's going on five days since I moved to Dublin. I found this bed-sit my first evening in town—a genuine feat in late-August Dublin, with a student population topping one hundred thousand. It's located on North side Dublin, Number One St. Alphonsus Road, in a section of town called Drumcondra.

Set my leather writing folder on the small table by the double doors, and step into my meager kitchen area to boil some potatoes. Take a turkey sandwich, bought earlier at a deli, from the refrigerator—the smallest fridge I have ever seen; holding six cans of beer and the sandwich, and not much else. Doesn't matter; this place is just a temporary stop, an address, a place to sleep—inarguable incentive to find work and move on.

Once the potatoes have boiled, I drain the water and pour a can of vegetable soup over them. Leave it on the burner another minute or two, then clear a space at the table. And I sit down to eat, listening to the evening news in the next room. It's unnerving living next to a man whose senses are so blunted that the news of the day must be screamed in his face.

I've heard some strange things in this house.

My second night I woke around midnight. Outside my door the landlady and her handyman boyfriend argued about his drinking—her staccato denunciations bandied back and forth with his lethargic, pitiable repetition, "Now wait a moment—just wait a moment now." They argued for twenty minutes before he slunk away, but I was up for hours afterward listening to the wind in the trees.

The next night I heard wailing. Not screaming or crying, but a human voice *wailing*. When I asked the landlady about it the next day, she said, "Oh, that was probably poor Sean, upstairs. He's deaf and dumb. What a yoke to bear. He sometimes gets frustrated not being able to speak, so he wails. He can't hear himself." Then her eyes widened, and she put her hand on my forearm. "He didn't disturb you, did he?"

I shook my head. "Just curious."

I haven't met the other two men living in the house. As yet my only contact with them has been hearing their footsteps pass my door, going to work in the mornings.

Having spent much of the morning seeing some of the old sights around town—St. Stephen's Green, Trinity College, Sinnot's pub, the Dublin Writers' Museum—then a few hours at the Writers' Centre, I am exhausted, and famished. I finish my dinner in minutes.

I wash my dishes as the light fades from the sky beyond the black security bars at my window, and feel the first shivering strands of homesickness unfurl—always at the quiet moments. While drying my pot and plate and fork, I find myself weighing this hovel against my parents' home; my dingy single bed to the futon and stereo and PC I left behind. Being here alone against being at home with my friends.

For Christ's sake, it's not like I'm going to be here forever. Just a temporary situation.

As I put away my pot and plate and fork, hang the

dishtowel over the handle on the oven door, I feel the pang, igniting the faces of my friends and family in my mind; surging their names to my lips.

I sit down with a novel I've been trying to read since arriving. Open the book knowing I won't make it to the bottom of the page. Thinking of home—Windsor, Ontario—feeling this pang that I have known for years, double-edged and incorrigible, gathering into a voice, bellowing through my nerves the ancient words God Himself used banishing Adam and Eve from the Garden of Eden, "Gird your loins and get the fuck out!"

I think about my father, John, who spent a year at the seminary. Imagining how he felt his first Saturday night there. Being twenty years old and hundreds of kilometers from his own bed in his widowed mother's home. This night, like the previous six, closes around the stone building of St. Peter's Divinity College, squeezing the breath from his lungs. In between the pulse of his queasy heart comes the voice of obligation, *A priest in the family. A priest in the family.*

It's his mother's wish that brought him to St. Peter's, mingled with his own vague sense of vocation, believing he might grow into religious life. But that has abandoned him tonight, replaced by a lonesome desolation taking hold with more force than his devotion to the Church ever has. But there should be no time for loneliness, the days are tightly ordered with studies, noon services in the chapel, meals, evening service, walks in the courtyard. Still, this fevered wondering worms its way in, *How did I get here? What am I doing here?* Followed by: *A priest in the family.*

He thinks of his friends: Pat McCormick borrowing his father's backfiring Studebaker, double-dating with Billy Strong. Going to Bowlero or the Pizza Parlor; Pat chain smoking, Billy's stutter worsening around the girls. Huddling together when their dates go to the bathroom, planning when and where to split up and go off with the girls to neck—by the waterfront, on the swings at the park.

He thinks of his best friend, Brian Gorman, driving his Chevrolet with Candace, his girlfriend of two years, going to the Skyway Drive-in or the Tastee-Freez for onion rings and vanilla Coke. Beneath the business of Brian's mind—figuring where to take Candace to neck, wondering if tonight she'll go all the way—there is an unfocused boredom, exhaustion with their hometown. Recalling conversations over beers at the Dominion House after work at the grocery store, Brian talking about leaving. Just driving away someday—for good. Then Candace came along and his plans broadened to include two.

"The seminary, huh?" Brian said when John first mentioned his decision to enroll. "No girls, no beer—can you live like that?"

"You think I'm nuts."

"Of course not. But the *priest*hood?"

"Ma thinks it's best," John said. "What's to keep me around here, anyway?"

"Won't be long before I hit the trail, too."

A wind rattles the windows and John's mind circles the neighborhoods, homes of friends and family. Imagines the Pizza Parlor, Bowlero, the Dominion House—the landscape of his life so familiar to him that he ceased seeing it. Lying in the dark, listening to the wind, they all light like beacons in his memory.

His thoughts turn to Paulette Roche, his girlfriend since tenth grade. Paulette—shy and proper, her pretty hair pinned-up in a bun. When talk of the seminary began, they went for walks by the river, often settling on a bench, watching the freighters float by. She would turn her eyes away, wring her hands and say nothing. The drift between them began months before the train ride to St. Peter's Divinity College. The silences grew weightier, awkward. No actual words of break-up were spoken. Paulette simply turned away. John stopped calling. Gradual as it had been, there was still the feeling of heartbreak.

Some nights after work John drove with Brian past her house, or walked by alone, looking for a light in her window.

Where is she tonight? On a date? Roller skating? At a movie with some guy's arm around her?

The wondering spirals into John's gut and the pang clenches tighter: *Maybe if I wrote her a letter and told her this is all a mistake, I'm sorry for leaving. Maybe she'd borrow her brother's car and come get me. But to tell Ma . . . the priests . . . .*

Wind presses against the windows. The sway of the autumn trees sounds like ocean surf. John opens his eyes to the dark, his breathing quick, near panic, thinking, *I got myself into this, I gotta get myself out.* And with the faces of his friends hovering above him, their names rising in his throat, John rolls over and tries to sleep.

And I see my mother, Kathleen, at age twenty-three—the year before she met my father—alone in the apartment she shares with her friend, Sylvia. Sylvia is working late, waitressing at the Pizza Parlor. April rain taps at the windows. Outside winter is loosening its grip, everything slush and mud, wet and dreary. She sits on the couch with a cup of tea, in a quilted dressing gown over her bedclothes. Stares at the blank TV screen.

She has been a social worker for almost a year. Although the difficulties and frustrations are balanced by small successes, there are nights like this, of quiet distraction, mulling the cases, the lives she sees unfolding, unraveling. Yesterday she took two young boys into care. They had no father and the mother was being sent to a sanitarium. Seemed no question about the mother's instability; the nurse at the boys' school was convinced, as was the justice of the peace and the ombudsman, who signed the committal papers. Before collecting the boys from school, Kathleen went to see their mother.

The moment she met the woman, Kathleen knew something was wrong. The woman came to the door doubled-over, clutching her abdomen, saying she was in tremendous pain. It seemed to Kathleen that the woman needed medical attention, no psychiatric care. After a short meeting, Kathleen went to collect the boys from school.

She took them out for hamburgers; tried to set them at ease. When she telephoned the office after eating, saying the boys were on their way to the Christian brothers' home, she received the news.

"The woman collapsed when the attendants arrived," her supervisor said. "They rushed her to the hospital. I guess she had a bleeding ulcer. She didn't make it."

It was left to Kathleen to tell the boys their mother had died.

While in traffic, on the way to the Christian brothers' home, the older boy opened the car door and tried to run away. Kathleen caught up to him, got him back into the car and brought them to the home.

And sitting in the empty apartment sipping her tea, she wonders about her friends, family—what are their concerns tonight?

There is Sylvia, getting married in a few months, her life filled with choosing silverware patterns, making lists for invitations, viewing houses with her fiancé. Kathleen's brother and sisters—they have their own families, lives. But to tell two young boys their mother has just died. The looks on their faces, wide startled eyes, their tears; the older boy trying to run away.

Where would he have gone? she wonders, hearing again the younger boy calling his brother's name. *How are they tonight? Did they have any appetite for dinner? How will they sleep? Where will they end up?*

The rain taps at the window, her tea goes cold. Kathleen stares at the blank TV screen, thinking of the cases yet to come.

The old basement still smells of fresh-cut wood and gasoline. A thousand tools are strewn through the workshop beyond the door, where the winter wood and snowmobiles are stored. It's cool as a cave; low ceiling with an I-beam overhead running the length of the room—we used to hang from it, see who could do the most pull-ups, hang from it the longest. Standing here again, my brother, Ben, can still hear the songs of Bryan Adams and Simple Minds blaring from a one-speaker cassette player, those nights we gathered in the Donald's darkened basement—Carolyn and Alyson, Robyn and Al; Frank, Jeff and Jodie. The songs emblazoned across the track of his memory.

Looks out the windows onto the hill sprawling down to the dock, which is constructed of logs and sodded, an extension of the lawn. Lake Chemong extends beyond it: reflecting the clear and cloudless late September sky. Evening has begun its slow creep over the horizon, casting everything in its mellow veil of orange and pink and purple.

It's a few weeks following his twenty-fourth birthday and Ben's come to visit old family friends—the Donalds, who live on Lake Chemong, a few kilometers outside of

Peterborough, Ontario. Our family once rented a cottage nearby, each summer for nine years. Frank and Jeff are still around. Ed, the eldest boy, is off working at a natural preserve as a park ranger. Jodie married a Marine and lives in the southern United States, the mother of two young sons.

It's been eleven years since we last went to the cottage. For only three weeks that final year, rather than the usual two months, as we did each previous summer. We left after only two weeks—the weather so cloudy and cold and sullen; there were only so many puzzles to do, only so many rounds of *Snake 'n' Ladders* or *Uno* we could bear to play.

Ben recalls the evening our parents decided to cut short that three-week stay. Larry Donald, our mother's old friend from the university, who had arranged the cottage for us, visited that night. Did his good-natured best to persuade us to stay, using all of his Irish charm to no avail. The weather was so ugly. In the end Larry gave a characteristic half-nod and wished us good night. Headed home in his old green fishing boat.

The following day Jeff Donald said to Ben, "What happened to Dad last night?"

Ben asked what he was talking about.

"He was crying when he got home."

Ben steps outside, along the flagstone path under the overhanging front porch. He looks up at the catwalk extending around the house. Recalls the day that Larry enlisted our help to build it. Three days it took, at the end of which Larry handed us each a beer—Ben was only eleven—saying, "If you're going to work like men, you may as well drink like men."

Ben goes down to the dock. There are a few fishermen on the lake heading in for the evening, a sailboat in the distance. There's no breeze and the water is flat as a pane of glass. Ben recalls how it used to fascinate and excite him, waking each summer morning, checking the lake first thing. The thrill of being the first to slice through that seamless surface on a slalom ski, warm as bath water after a night of rain.

He looks at the blue V-hull Crestliner roped in its well. Old Blue. The boat once towed seven skiers simultaneously. Back in the days of two skis.

Ben first slalom skied when he was seven—one of his water skis accidentally came off of his foot and he managed to keep his balance. He barefoot water-skied when he was twelve, following an uncountable procession of head jarring tumbles at full-throttle. He was shaky that first time up, gasping for air through the tremendous spray fanning up over his toes. Pulled the baton close to his chest, spread his legs apart—the spray cutting an eight-foot-high V behind him—the look of startled concentration on his face breaking into a grin.

A pickup truck pulls into the driveway at the top of the hill in a flourish of flying gravel. Frank Donald and his friend, Al Green, step out. Grinning, Frank jogs down the hill calling Ben's name.

"Mom called work and said you were here already," Frank says, shaking his hand. Al slaps Ben on the shoulder and shakes his hand.

"We just finished dinner," Ben says. "She hooked Jeff into helping with the dishes."

"Good," Frank says. "What do you say about a ski?"

"What? Now?" Ben says. "It's getting dark."

"There's always time for one last ski."

"We'll tape a flashlight around your neck if it'll make you feel better," Al says and winks.

"Well, do you have a suit for me?" Ben asks.

"Sure," says Frank as he and Al step into Old Blue. There is a pile of life vests and a couple of wet suits in the bow of the boat.

"The spray coming up between your legs is so powerful," Ed Donald, water-ski guru of Lake Chemong, had once explained, "that it can go all the way up your ass and tear out your guts if you're not wearing a wet suit."

Frank tosses a wet suit on the dock. Al slides a slalom ski on the dock and unties the boat as Frank starts the engine. The roar startles Ben. It always has.

Frank reverses out of the well and circles around the dock.

Breathing the familiar odor of the engine exhaust, Ben pulls on the wet suit and fastens it at the shoulder. Slips his foot into the slalom ski and stands at the edge of the dock—four feet above the water—ski extended before him, ready to take off like we always have. Al throws him the towrope baton.

The boat drifts away from the dock. When the slack of the towrope is almost taken up, Ben shouts, "Hit it!"

Frank throws the boat's throttle forward and Old Blue lurches in the water. Ben leaps off the dock, landing heavily on the ski. His balance falters for a moment, but as the boat planes-out he straightens and puts his right foot into the holster on the back of the ski. Frank veers to the left past the small tree-choked island, toward the horseshoe-shaped ring of land called Fife's Bay.

Ben speeds over the wake, pulls back on the towrope. Cuts back. It's been at least two years since he skied; he cuts a little too sharply. His balance falters, but recovers.

Entering Fife's Bay, Frank has Old Blue going full-tilt. Ben moves over the boat's narrowing wake. Slides his right foot out of the holster, digging his heel into the water. He leans back, feeling the pull of muscles through his shoulders, arms, back and hips. Leans further back until he nearly at a forty-five degree angle above the water. Then he kicks off the ski, digging the other heel into the water.

The spray coming up from his feet is ferocious, filling

his mouth and eyes, going up his nose. Turns his head, bends his knees, pulls the baton closer to his chest, spreading his legs apart. The spray lowers to his midriff and he can breathe again.

Al shakes his fist above his head, cheering him on. Frank kneels on the driver's seat, watching over his shoulder.

Ben eases across the wake, over to the right as Frank follows the contour of the bay. The water is slick and firm under his feet. Friends who saw him barefoot a few years ago asked if it hurt.

"It doesn't hurt," Ben said. "The water vibrates against your feet. If you go long enough it almost tickles."

Moving along the shoreline past all of those empty docks, seeing the covered boats on their lifts, the darkened windows of cottages, Ben feels some of the old sadness that came when it was time to go home each year. More than summer's end, more than the dread of school starting. Even years ago, somewhere in his adolescent mind was the knowledge, the mourning of time passing. With every summer that passed, the lake changed a little.

Ed's gone. Ed, who used to barefoot water-ski backwards; who never let go of the towrope. He would fall, bounce across the water, holding onto the baton with one hand. Then roll onto his back, spin around on his buttocks and stand up again. People used to fight over who would spot for Ed, because he was better than anything you'd see on a television sports show.

Jodie's gone. Sweet and simple, pretty and hospitable, Jodie was a constant good friend. Now married. Now a mother. And very sorely missed.

Carolyn and Alyson, and the rest of the friends who still occasionally visit the lake. They have drifted, busy with other pursuits in other cities: university degrees, marriages, jobs.

Inevitable.

As Frank rounds back for home, closing-in on the dock, he makes a hard turn left, and the tug of velocity breaks Ben's reverie. He lets go of the baton, glides a few yards and sinks into the water. Frank goes back to retrieve the slalom ski. Al stands in the boat's stern, reeling in the towrope.

Ben swims to the dock knowing he will be stiff and sore tomorrow—the muscles in his arms, legs and back crucified with tonight's effort. But as the muscles scream the next day and the day after that, he will savor it. Remembering.

I put my book down. It's too early to sit still, to be alone. I grab my jacket and go around the corner to Quinn's Pub.

It's Tuesday night and the place is empty. I order a pint, step away from the bar and place my pint on the platform ringing a wooden pillar. The TVs mounted on the walls are on, but a CD plays on the sound system, so I watch the news imagining what's being said. And with unstoppable regularity, I think about home, my friends. Wishing Craig and Dan and Lewis, Mike and Jen were here with me. Wonder what Dennis and Mira are doing tonight.

Wish my brother was here with me.

Think back to the thousand times I was asked by friends and family and acquaintances: Why leave Canada? Why Ireland? Why now? And the voice of the pang ringing through me, "Gird your loins and get the fuck out!" Feeling exhilaration and doubt, excitement and fear—half-a-hundred emotions leaving me unsure just how I felt. The only thing sure was the sense to leave. To write. To work. Go someplace where I wouldn't feel so stale.

Sipping my pint I hear the commotion of a group coming into the pub, ordering their drinks. I look over my shoulder and see five or six people arranging a circle of stools. I listen to the CD that's playing, watch the flash of pictures on the television set. Look at my watch: 7:47 p.m—going on three in the afternoon back at home.

And I remember:

A staff Christmas party for a part-time job two years before, where I liberally abused the free-bar in the boss's house only to berate a room full of bewildered high school students about Irish history: Brian Boru with a sword in each hand. How Boru—who had been king of Ireland back in the late Tenth Century A.D.—had driven away the Vikings, who vastly outnumbered him and his men. Then, upon returning to his tent to fix his hair and listen to Elvis Presley records, was beheaded by some runaway Viking . . . That night blurring to blackness as I was carried to a waiting taxi.

Waking the following day with a colossal hangover—guts feeling like they had stewed in sauerkraut; sweating and gasping, wondering if my health was gone entirely.

Recalling: Winning a writing competition, and being taken out by a good buddy and an old girlfriend to celebrate. Going to the river front with a cooler of beer and sandwiches wrapped in waxed paper. We drank among the shadows, looking at the Detroit train yards across the water, marveling how the lights of the Ambassador Bridge looked like a string of pearls. By night's end, the beer gone, glowing, gratefully drunk, I tied the bed sheet we had been sitting on around my neck, and ran down the hill to the paved walk, declaring myself *MATTMAN*.

The people behind me in Quinn's Pub burst out laughing, goading one another to sing a song. The pub is cavernous and voices carry with startling clarity. After a moment a man begins singing in a loud, cigarette-ravaged voice.

I recall going with friends to St. Andrew's Hall in Detroit to see Shane MacGowan in concert. I wore my Sawney Beane

T-shirt—a band led by a good friend of mine; a loyal devotee of MacGowan's. Sitting, sweating in St. Andrew's that July night, I had finished my tenth or eleventh beer by the time MacGowan finally slouched onstage. Halfway through the show I left my seat in the upper tier, went around to the side. Pulled off my Sawney Beane shirt—a silhouette silkscreen of the band with their Celtic instruments—balled it up and hurled it at the stage. I was aiming for MacGowan's head but hit the bass player, instead. There was a hitch in the song, as the musicians reacted to something being thrown onstage. MacGowan teetered forward, stooping for the shirt, but a roadie scurried onto the stage, retrieving it first.

Watching the TV in Quinn's Pub, the group behind me goes on laughing and singing. I finish my pint and order another. A song comes over the sound system, slow and sweet, a woman's voice rising to piercing heights. Which is followed a moment later by up-tempo music. I'm not sure about the music, but the woman sounds great. Straining to hear the singing I think to ask the barman what CD is playing. I turn to get up—and stop. The woman singing is sitting behind me, among that group. She's no more than twenty, perched atop her stool, legs crossed, her back against the bar, eyes closed. Singing a wonderful, lilting song I've never heard before.

When she finishes, her friends applaud and call for another song from another singer. As some someone else shares his song, I look back at the television screen across the pub without seeing it. Whisper the names of my friends and family as my missing begins to ebb.

For a while.

And the Rocks and Stones Shall Sing

It was Saturday night, and the usual commotion of drunks and police sirens were heard beyond these Dublin City council flats. Christy Wallace, caretaker of the Father O'Faolain flats, got up from the late-night movie he was watching on RTÉ One, and shuffled into the kitchen for a final shot of whisky. Setting down the bottle, he heard the first crash.

"What the hell—?" Christy grunted, startled.

He shuffled to the front window of his ground level flat. In the front of the building stood a young man before the sun-faded statue of Jesus Christ. The statue was four feet tall, mounted atop a concrete pedestal within a Plexiglas case, arms outstretched. The young man had a brick—drew his arm back and launched it at the case.

Crash!

Christy looked at the clock on the mantle, barely visible in the flickering light of the television. Quarter past one.

The third crash came and Christy's wife called from the bedroom, "What in God's name is going on out there?"

"Some drunk's attacking Christ out the front."

"What?"

"Go back to sleep." He sipped his whisky.

"Are you calling the police?"

"It's Saturday night—it'll be daylight before they get around here."

"Well, don't go out there yourself."

"I won't," Christy snapped. He was sixty-two and caretaker of the building. "He'll tire and go away."

I hope, Christy thought and swallowed the rest of his

whisky.

Crash!

He poured himself another drink and moved a chair over to the front window.

After the pub and a spell at a friend's flat, Adam was headed back to his own place. Passing through this neighborhood he noticed it across the street: the statue of Jesus Christ. He had seen it before, months ago, when he first moved to Dublin; it was along his route to the Irish Writers' Centre. And the irony was too much, writing to friends and family back in Canada—*Jesus in a plastic bubble. Not even the Lord is safe in this neighborhood.* And forgot about it.

He crossed the street and approached the statue, wondering, *Maybe the case is to protect it from the weather.* And remembered the story of Christ calming the storm. *Maybe it's protection from vandals.* And recalled the stories of Jesus sitting down to eat with tax collectors and prostitutes.

And vandals would likely just smash the statue. And suddenly saw in his memory the thousand grisly depictions of Golgotha from countless religion classes through years of attending Roman Catholic schools.

He went over to a short, crumbling wall and kicked away one of the loose bricks. The brick had a good weight to it; there was an unspoken seriousness about its solidity: you can't take lightly a man with a brick in his hand.

Adam approached the case—his eyes level with Christ's ankles—and hurled the brick at the center of case, causing a loud, reverberating crash. The Plexiglas cracked. He picked the brick up and threw it again. All the while he was aware of lights going on in the surrounding cluster of council flats.

"Hey, there," a woman called. "Keep that up and the police will be called."

Adam plucked the broken Plexiglas from the frame in large, jagged pieces. By the time he removed the entire front pane, there were people standing on balconies and looking out windows. He stared up at the four-foot Christ with its arms outstretched; the gesture appeared more a plea than an offer of redemption.

With an audience of wakened, baffled onlookers Adam shouted at the four-foot tall statue, "Jesus, arise!"

Nothing happened.

"That's not drink," one voice said. "That's madness."

He shouted again, "Jesus, *arise!*"

The statue stood staring from within its protective case.

Adam turned away, turned his eyes to those standing on their balconies, watching through windows. "All right, then," he said, his voice echoing down the narrow lane. "*Every*one, arise!"

Christy put his empty glass on the kitchen counter. He thought about pouring one last shot of whisky before going outside to survey the damage to the statue. It was going on half-past one and the drunk had finally gone away.

Jesus arise! Christy thought. Every*one arise!* "What the hell's that about?" he muttered, putting on his jacket and going outside.

The front pane of the case was completely broken away, but the statue itself was unharmed. *Where am I going to get another piece of Plexiglas this time of night?* Christy wondered. *And tomorrow Sunday. Jaysus.*

The statue of Jesus stared out at the cool night.

"And now for somebody to steal the damned thing," Christy grunted. *Who'd take care of a thing like that—replace it?* he wondered. *The Church? The City?*

He wasn't sure; he had lived and worked ten years in the

building, but the statue had been there longer.

And now for somebody to steal it . . .

As Christy gathered up the large pieces of Plexiglas from the ground and went inside, an idea came to him. Smiling to himself, he went into the kitchen and dropped the broken Plexiglas into the rubbish bin. Then he grabbed a roll of cellophane. Took his stepladder from the closet.

With care and a sense of outwitting the criminal element of Dublin, Christy wrapped the Plexiglas case with cellophane. When he was finished the statue of Jesus was a blurred, indistinguishable form within. But it was a good job . . . *and pretty damned clever, too,* Christy thought. *Ah, but nobody cares about that kind of thing anymore.* He shook his head. *All sorts of things nobody gives a damn about anymore.*

His satisfaction did not falter. Christy gave the statue a final look before going into the building. "Let the bastard come back now with his brick."

Journey to the Gate

My time in Ireland was spent following impulse like it was good sense, visiting parks and pubs, exploring one end of the River Liffey to the other, and working on my book at the Irish Writers' Centre. I lost whole days walking Raglan Road where Patrick Kavanagh once lived and set his famous poem, drinking in Ryan's where the American poet John Berryman composed an avalanche of Dream Songs, losing afternoons and evenings in the myriad pubs where Brendan Behan wrote, drank, sang and was barred. Or, reclining with a book on the shaded grounds of St. Stephen's Green, site of public executions in centuries past.

The Saturday I embarked on the pilgrimage was the sort of day for which Ireland doesn't get credit: bright and warm, the sky a great blue slab rubbed clear of clouds. Dublin City Centre thronged with pedestrians by ten a.m. With my backpack over my shoulder, I rode the southbound DART train beyond the city limits, through Dun Loaghaire, Dalkey, and Sandycove. Passing over Grand Canal Basin and Ringsend Road, I glimpsed Windmill Lane Studios, and recalled the day I spent searching for that unmarked, warehouse-like building, all sooty and sullied by the exhaust of passing traffic. It stood next to a garage where city buses were repaired, and was where artists like U2 and Sinead O'Connor recorded albums.

When I tried the windowless front door, it was locked.

I pressed the intercom button.

"Yes?" a female voice crackled over the speaker.

"Courier," I said, wondering from where that reply came. Then I heard the snap of the automatic lock-release.

Stepping through the door was like crossing a threshold:

from the traffic-choked drear of Ringsend Road into the Sanctum. Where my heroes trod. The place was plush: rich carpeting flowed from the foyer into the reception area, like the map of an ancient river. The foyer walls were white plaster sloping round-edged into the ceiling, cozy and cave-like. Inside the panelled reception area, the place smelled of cedar and polish and perfume. The receptionist was a girl no more than twenty, blue-eyed, pert and pretty in her grey blazer and mint-green blouse. The wall behind her was adorned with gold and platinum records, most belonging to U2. Rock music played on hidden speakers.

I noticed a door in the far right-hand corner. Closed. *There,* I thought, sure of it. *Behind that door is where it happens—where they record.* Who was in there now? Would the door open any moment and Bono and the boys stride past me on their way to lunch?

The receptionist seemed to smile and frown at the same time—I didn't resemble the couriers riding motorcycles, swaggering into buildings clad in black nylon, or leather rain-gear; helmets balanced atop their heads in tenuous compliance with the *COURIERS PLEASE REMOVE HELMETS* signs posted at most office entrances.

"Can I help you," she said.

"I'm a Canadian," I said. Then the mischievous deity, who prompted the lie that got me through the door, swooped to my aid. I said, "I'm a Canadian, and a courier of sorts."

I was carrying my leather writing folder, which contained a city map, a notebook, postcards I had yet to write—and a CD recorded by friends from Windsor, Ontario, who played in a Celtic rock band. Took more than a year to record, mix and press, and was sold by drunken lackeys from shoeboxes at bars during their shows. I had brought it to banish the homesickness.

I presented the CD to the receptionist.

"Sawney Beane," she said, reading the cover. "What's that?"

"The band," I said. "The name comes from a tenth century Scottish cannibal."

She stared at me.

I shrugged. "The guys are Scottish history buffs."

"We're not an agency, just a recording studio."

"Well, I promised the guys I'd deliver it *some*where," I said, and turned to go.

The receptionist seemed relieved.

Moving through the foyer, looking at the abstract art on the walls, I noticed the music over the hidden speakers had stopped. A moment later came the familiar strains of Sawney Beane's "The Grad House Song." I opened the door and stepped back out to the overcast day. The windowless door slammed behind me. The lock caught immediately.

Mass transportation always lulls me, the cradle-rock of the train on the uneven track, and the blur of landscape passing before my eyes like a hypnotist's trick. Swaying with the train's motion, I thought about the Wall. It was located near the original Windmill Lane Studios, where U2 recorded their first three albums. The studio had moved to Ringsend Road in the mid-1980's, and the group continued to record at the new facility. Old-time fans went to the original studio, adding graffiti to the Wall, which had become an illegible mass of tributes written in more languages than I could name. Adoration gone unintelligible.

Twenty minutes into the journey the train rounded onto the coastal mountain. No matter how often I rode the DART, this always took me by surprise: rounding a bend, coming out of land-locked suburban monotony to find the train several hundred feet above the Irish Sea—confronted by a wide-open scene of water and mountains and beach and sky and sky and sky.

Killiney Bay.

I felt nervous thinking of what lay ahead, and gripped my backpack. The right-brained pragmatist in me swelled with embarrassment, uncertainty, thinking, This is stupid. It was the same doubt I often felt about my book while writing at the lopsided table of my bed-sit, or sitting before a PC at the Irish Writers' Centre. Wondering if moving to Dublin was the only way I could get an objective view of my hometown, or if anyone would care about my book even if I ever finished writing it. And then second-guessing the pilgrimage.

Did I actually believe I would be arrested?

No.

Or, worried others would be present, and that I might be too self-conscious to go through with my spiritual errand? I nodded over that. But that wasn't it, entirely. It was the apprehension of setting out to fulfill a dream: fear that what had seemed miraculous and unattainable might be rendered all too earthly upon closer inspection—like the sooty structure of Windmill Lane Studios.

I got off at the Killiney DART station, a forlorn little place, like a lost telegraph station in a corner of Eastern Europe. Passing through the turnstiles, heading outside, my breathing quickened, my heart rate was up. I struck out to the right, up Station Road. The Killiney Court Hotel was on my left, and the sea beyond the DART tracks was to the right. A few hundred yards up the way, Station Road turned ninety degrees to the left, then veered again to the right, inclining up a steep hill.

Toward Vico Road.

And I pondered how steep climbs were usually involved in pilgrimages. Thinking of St. Kevin amid the dense forest of Sixth Century Glendalough, scaling a forbidding rock face in order to meditate, and evade a woman in pursuit of him. The woman, legend has it, climbed up to his nook, and soon after plunged to her death when St. Kevin cast her out. Until recent years, pilgrimages were led up that rock face. That cast-out woman was now a footnote, an anecdote recounted by tour guides around the ancient chapel in Glendalough, known as St. Kevin's Kitchen. When I first heard it, years ago, I was less intrigued by St. Kevin and his venerators than his poor, doomed pursuer. The first of his pilgrims, it could be said. Rejected. Cast out.

The area was heavily wooded, branches interlacing over the road. A seven-foot-tall stone wall ran along either side of the sloping road. Although the day was bright, the air smelled of dank stone, moldering moss, and damp tree bark. Aside from birds singing back and forth, there was heavy silence; nothing indicating human presence—no lawn mower drone, no car engine, or voices, or even music from a portable radio. I was soon out of breath with the climb.

The first sign of habitation was the wrought-iron gates fronting a white stucco estate. Through the bars of the gate I saw lush green grounds, and the Irish Sea in the distance. A bronze plaque gleamed next to the gate: *UNDERCLIFF.* I continued up the incline, my shoulder and back perspiring beneath my bag. Rounding a bend in the road, I first glimpsed the Gate.

I stopped. Stared. Awed.

In a world abounding with sacred places—Giza,

Golgotha, Graceland, *Cimetiere du Pere-Lachaise*—none was more hallowed to me than Vico Road, Killiney, County Dublin.

The road widened here, allowing in sunshine. Ivy clung in regal green patches to the stone wall. Daisies dotted the tall grass by the road.

The gate stood approximately ten feet high and fifteen feet wide; wrought iron, backed with copper panels, and duly imposing. Approaching it, everything within me tensed, quivering like an arrow striking its target. The mansion was not visible from the road. That didn't matter. I came to see the gate fronting the estate of Paul Hewson, formerly of Ballymun, North Dublin. Better known as Bono.

I had heard about the gate from my friend, Ronan. He read a news article when it was first installed.

"What's newsworthy about a celebrity putting in a large gate," I'd said.

"It's covered with Bono's writing."

"How's that?"

"Etched right into the copper—lyrics and drawings, the whole lot. Supposed to be a love letter to his fans, or some shite."

The copper panels were immense, dull as a worn penny, but not yet green from the elements. The entire expanse was covered with writing: poems and drawings, throwaway lines, entire passages. The top of one panel read *EVERYTHING YOU KNOW IS WRONG.*

Below it:

In the service of God one can learn three things from a child and seven from a thief. From a child one can learn 1) always be happy 2) never to sit idle 3) and cry for everything one wants.

From a thief you should learn 1) to work at night 2) if one can-
not gain it in one night to try again the next night 3) to love one's
co-workers just as thieves love each other 4) to be willing to risk
one's life even for a little thing 5) not to attach too much value to
things even though you've risked your life for them just as a thief
will resell a stolen article for a fraction of its worth 6) to with-
stand all kinds of beatings and tortures but to remain what you
are and 7) to believe that your work is worthwhile and not be
willing to change it.

There was an etching of a butcher's knife. Above it read
VISION AND PRAYER. The rest of the panel was adorned
with images of wrenches, pliers, a screwdriver, paintbrush,
scissors, a newborn baby wailing. Along another panel I read
I HAVE SPREAD MY DREAMS AT YOUR FEET. Other passages were written in Spanish and French.

My gaze swept back and forth, wanting to see everything
at once. The writing was no larger than you'd find in a notebook. And I recalled as a kid reading *No One Here Gets Out*
Alive, the biography of Jim Morrison, and wondering over the
naked thrill of possessing some ordinary scrap of Morrison's
life: a postcard written by him, his driver's license, drafts of his
writing. Then, coming across the lyrics to "L.A. Woman," in
the book, written in Morrison's hand, was like discovering the
Dead Sea Scrolls.

I placed my hands on the panels, pressing my palms
against the writing. And thought of a Ray Bradbury story,
where a vacationing American—sometime in the 1950's—is
travelling with his wife in Southern France. He is a Picasso
enthusiast excited about spending a few days in "Picasso
country." That evening, strolling an empty beach he notices
a solitary figure by the shoreline, drawing in the sand with a
stick. Curious, the American approaches. And finds it is

Pablo Picasso. He says nothing to the artist, not wanting to distract him from the panoramic, mesmerizing mural he draws in the sand; images, familiar and grotesque, woven together in a dizzying array. When the American finally looks up, Picasso wishes him good night and departs, walking down the beach, toward the south. The man looks from the artist to the work, awed and horrified, knowing the wind and high tide will soon claim it—no way to take even the barest bit of it away with him.

The first rock concert I ever attended was to see Bob Dylan. I was fifteen. Since then I've seen most of my favorites: U2, Lou Reed, Stevie Ray Vaughn, among others. However, the greatest rock 'n' roll moment I ever witnessed occurred in the summer of 1985: watching Live Aid on TV.

I was fourteen, and had been playing guitar for a couple of years, steeping myself in rock 'n' roll mythology: reading Jim Morrison's biography, *'Scuse Me While I Kiss the Sky,* the biography of Jimi Hendrix, *Neil and Me,* by Neil's father, Scott Young. I discovered the film and soundtrack to *Woodstock*, 1969, the previous year. However, Live Aid was the first musical Happening of my life. I waited with keen anticipation to see Led Zeppelin and The Who—both reuniting for the event—along with Bob Dylan, Neil Young, Santana. Before any of them took the stage, U2 played.

I was home, strumming my guitar, paying little attention to U2's performance until Bono launched into the chorus of their song "Bad"—his voice gathering like a storm, filling Wembley Stadium: ocean surf crashing upon shore. I marveled at the power, the plea in it.

Soon after, Bono dropped the microphone to the stage, and walked away.

As the band played, he jumped down to the platform

where television cameras filmed the concert. He ran past a cameraman, and surveyed the massive audience.

I set my guitar aside, watching.

Bono waved his arms in a beckoning gesture, calling the crowd forward. He stopped. Seemed flustered, frustrated by the enormity of the audience. Then he bent over the platform's guardrail, pointing into the crowd. Pointed, and brought both hands to his chest. Pointed and gestured to himself, singling someone out. Again and again, saying with his emphatic movements, "Her. Bring *her* to me."

A gasp rippled through the audience when Bono climbed over the guardrail, and dropped into the moat between the security fence and the base of the stage. Three members of the security staff, in yellow T-shirts, worked to extract a young woman from the mob writhing at the fence. Photographers swarmed in.

When the young woman was pulled free, she threw herself into Bono's arms.

And there, amid the tumult of security, photographers—garbage strewn on the ground from the crowd along the fence—the screaming multitudes thronging the field and filling the surrounding stands, Bono danced with the girl. Eyes closed. Holding her hand, holding her close, as though alone in a quiet pub, moving to a favourite song.

I watched, transfixed, breath caught in my throat, a flash of tears searing my eyes. I was only fourteen, didn't know much about much, but always sensed there was more to rock 'n' roll than electric guitars and long hair; more than just *entertainment*—and had just seen proof of that.

Bono kissed the girl, then climbed back up to the TV camera platform. He took up the microphone again, and filled Wembley—filled me—with his voice.

* * *

Poring over the panels, I noticed the security camera built into the stone wall, and knew why it was there: December 8th, 1980, "Mr. Lennon, can I have your autograph?"

I thought how most fans lead ordinary lives of quiet admiration, buying their favourite artists' work—attending concerts, film premieres, book signings, art exhibitions. Enjoying the work and maybe loving it, and by extension, loving the artist—be he Lennon, Dali, Joyce, or simply Paul Hewson. Not all hero worship was lunging to pull a handful of 1964-John-Lennon's hair as he runs through a gauntlet of maniacal teenagers. We didn't all want to leave our mark with spray paint or bullets. Gone, however, were the days of Bono inviting fans into his home. I understood why adulation made most celebrities uncomfortable—it's something blind, aimed at its target like a cannon.

My parents visited Ireland the year before, and we spent a week driving to Donegal. On the way back to Dublin, we made a side-trip to Knock, site of a visitation of the Holy Family in 1879, and since made a national shrine. We went more out of curiosity than anything else. Everybody has his own religion, though not all of us can fit it into a church.

We went into the glassed-in chapel where a perpetual mass was said, on the very ground of the original visitation. Walked along the bigger-than-life statuary depicting the Stations of the Cross. Photographed the giant cross at the far end of the grounds. Entered the larger chapel where Pope John Paul II had celebrated Eucharist in 1979. We even bought bottles to fill at the outdoor holy water fonts: a row of taps jutting above cement embossings with the particular cures and turns of good luck they brought—holy water to bless travellers, musicians, farmers, the blind, the arthritic.

The official grounds of Knock were tranquil, well tended.

Ten yards outside it were rows of shops with names like "St. Martin's Souvenirs," selling trinkets, like the junk found in the back pages of comic books: plastic dashboard statues of saints, key chains, posters, place-mats, dishes and lawn statues, all emblazoned with the faces of the Holy Family. Put me in mind of a friend who had visited Rome years ago telling me about booths near the Vatican selling Shroud of Turin dish-towels. Adoration gone unintelligible.

As with every first kiss and last breath, the moment ended. Much as I mourned leaving that gate, I hadn't come to take away some piece of Bono, but to read his love letter, and leave my own.

I opened my backpack and withdrew the manuscript I had been writing since moving to Ireland—an Augustinian account of my reckless years in Windsor, Ontario: boozy rampages, the thousand hung over mornings, friends gained, lost and gone, people I missed, and our adventures together. In letters to friends I described the manuscript as a 300-page Haiku, a hundred thousand-word soul song. Having shown it to no one, I had yet to decide whether I ever would.

I attached a note thanking Bono for his song "All I Want Is You," and apologizing "for any distress caused by the flight my flaming-arrow-manuscript" over his wall. Then, wishing him peace and happiness with his family and in his work, signed it "Good luck and Godspeed."

And hurled my manuscript over the gate.